Murder in the Hare Meadow

The Wootton Windmill Mysteries
Book 5

Izzie Harper

ASIN for the ebook: B0CNY2F2WX

ISBN for the paperback: 978-1-7392189-4-2

For Stacy Hanley and Liberty's Pet Services

and

Catherine Kirk and White Mill Vets

for going 'above and beyond' when Lexi and I both had surgery.

Chapter 1
SATURDAY

When Ellie Blix woke up, she was in a strange bed in an unfamiliar room with something chewing her hair. She raised her hand to feel what it was. Paws encircled her fingers, and a soft mouth gripped them.

The kittens were awake.

There was another at the nape of her neck, and one on her stomach. At her feet, a further three were rolling around on the duvet, showing off their beautiful stripes and soft, creamy bellies.

She switched her alarm off and sat up, careful not to dislodge any of her furry charges. Tabitha, the mother, was fast asleep on the floor in the basket, purring loudly.

It was the week before Easter and behind the shutters, the spring sun shone brightly. Lower Wootton Pets was in the high street, four doors down from the butcher's. In an hour and a half, the pet shop staff would be arriving downstairs to open up. Today was going to be busy: a litter of baby rabbits had been delivered yesterday, and there was a list of excited buyers coming in.

But Ellie had a few minutes before she needed to get up. Usually, at this time in the morning, she was waking in a busy home, letting Rebus out for his morning dash round the garden, checking the rota in her cleaning business' diary and fighting her daughter and mother-in-law for the bathroom.

This was a taste of a different life. No family for a couple of hours; no business to run. A bathroom to herself.

Ellie stroked one of the kittens. Its bright eyes shone. Tiny, innocent face, whiskers so fine she could barely see them. Unsteady on its feet, tail erect. 'Was it you doing zoomies at 2am?'

The kitten raised a front paw and promptly collapsed into a heap.

'Careful, little one.'

Another kitten joined them. Smaller. Swaying slightly and more tentative, stopping at intervals and splaying its feet. Hiding behind folds of duvet and peering over.

'Hello, you.'

Ellie let the kitten approach. Then a third. Bigger and bolder. Pushed itself forward and rolled on its back, waving chubby paws in the air, seemingly unsure which bits belonged to him.

On the bedside table, another bundle of mischief was pawing the charging lead, which was loose. The kitten was leaping about like it wasn't in control of its body, arching its back and pouncing on a 'snake' in a tiny jungle.

Over at the shutters, another kitten was fully extended, a mass of stripes, desperately reaching for the long, white cord.

Ellie shuffled over to the window and peered through the semi-open slats. Hopefully, Francesca, the pet shop owner, would be back from her mother's soon and Ellie could return home to her own menagerie and family and routine. Fran's mother had slipped while putting out the bin, and had broken her hip. Fran was visiting her in hospital and doing post-op care until her brother arrived from Spain.

From the bedroom window, two storeys above the pet shop, the high street was waking from its slumber. To the left, the light was on at the florist and the owner was already putting trays of daffodils and tulips outside; bags of donations lay in piles in the doorway of the charity shop.

It was a different view from her usual one at the converted windmill where she lived. Here at the shop, she saw the pale green front of the vet's opposite, blinds drawn across huge wooden windows; the white fascia of the dentist's, yellow jonquils bobbing in window boxes; the doctor's surgery to the right, double fronted and a gleaming white. Along the edge of the road, three dark grey cherry plums were a mass of white flowers.

Her gaze drifted to the pedestrian crossing. Two runners came into view, striding out on the spring morning. Their chatter floated, barely audible but a reminder of human life and company.

Ellie was putting Tabitha's food in her bowl when her phone rang in the other room. She needed to get it in case it was one of her cleaners phoning in sick. As soon as the call rang off, it started again... and a third time after that. Someone must want her urgently.

She shut Tabitha and the kittens in the kitchen – as per Fran's instructions – and went to retrieve her mobile.

Three missed calls from Zoe.

She dialled her daughter's number.

'I'll WhatsApp-video you,' came Zoe's voice, unusually brusque for her, before she rang off and redialled.

Full of anticipation, Ellie accepted the video call. Zoe had either seen some wildlife or got a good shot on her camera for the photography competition.

The video frame opened, and she saw lush spring grass, a large area of water, a weeping willow... and a white-faced Zoe, eyes wide with alarm.

'There's a body in the pond,' Zoe blurted, her voice quaking.

'What? You mean, a human one?'

'Yeah. I didn't see it at first. There were two hares, boxing. I followed them when they shot off and saw it then. Look.' She turned the camera round on her phone.

Ellie ran cold all over.

A mass was protruding out of the water, head lying back, nose, stomach and two feet peeping above the surface.

'Good grief. Have you rung the police?'

'Yeah. They're on their way.'

Ellie's mind was racing. 'It's potentially a crime scene so don't go any closer.'

'I won't. Don't worry.' Zoe zoomed in on her phone camera so they could see the body better. 'It's a man.'

'Hang on.' Ellie screwed up her eyes to get a better look. 'Is that a tattoo beneath his ear?'

'Yeah. A black anchor. Seems familiar, don't know where from.'

It had red handles on each side and a yellow ribbon round the main bar.

'I recognise it. From the newspaper and the TV. It's the bloke who's just been released from prison. Lloyd Durden.'

Chapter 2

An hour later, Ellie was driving home through the village, with the kittens and Tabitha in their carry-case in the back of the jeep.

She barely knew Lloyd Durden but couldn't get him out of her mind. His release from prison had stirred up the village, only two years after his conviction for running down their beloved 'lollipop lady' on the pelican crossing by the school. Understandably, there had been a lot of objection to him returning home to live. Even though his father *insisted* his son had served his time and was sorry for what he'd done, feelings were running high again.

For Lloyd to end up dead in the pond, though? It was a shock. Surely, he hadn't been murdered?

They didn't know yet how he'd died, but he was well known for his drinking. Perhaps he'd gone on a bender and fallen in? Or had a heart attack and collapsed into the water?

In the high street, Ellie was relieved to shift her focus to the village shops, which were beginning to open. She loved this time of day. Seeing the village wake up and regain its energy. Watching friends and neighbours go about their lives and businesses.

A few doors down from the pet shop, Charlie Matthews was putting a chalk board outside the butcher's, publicising their deals of the day. Free range pork loin; farm reared sirloin steaks; their own sausages. With his dark, floppy hair, white butcher's coat, and warm smile, he was a charismatic figure.

'Morning,' she said to him through her open car window.

He was only a few feet away and waved at her.

'We tried your new range last week. The pancetta. Sylvia put it in a shepherd's pie. Delicious.'

'Nice one. I'll tell Dad.'

His father, Nick, was one of Ellie's old schoolfriends.

At the hairdresser's, Helen was raising the blinds.

Ellie made an "I'll phone you" gesture. She and Helen had been talking about a night out for ages.

The window of the baker's was a bright array of colours. The owner had displayed the eggs the local schoolchildren had painted for Easter before term ended. Next to these was the giant yellow chick that the owner's daughter had made.

Outside, a huge poster was tied to the railings.

"Come along to the LOWER WOOTTON BUNNY HOP – family fun on Easter Sunday," it said.

Zoe was taking her jacket off when Ellie got back to the windmill and let herself in. The beautiful building had been in Ellie's family for several generations, going back to the days when it was used to mill cereals from the fields. To the Blix family now, it was home.

Rebus flung himself at Ellie, having not seen her all night, oblivious of the carry-case and mewling cargo.

'Mind, boy. Let me put this lot down and I can say hello properly.' She took the kittens into the office and got them settled. 'We'll leave their case and litter tray in there so we can shut the door when we need to,' she told Zoe, 'and let them out when we're around. That's what Fran said to do.'

'Leave it open now then,' said Zoe. 'We're all here.'

'OK.' Ellie left the door ajar. 'We've got to remember: there are six of them, plus Tabitha.' She smiled. It wasn't easy because they all looked so similar.

'When's Fran back at the shop?'

'In a few days. She rang last night. Her mum's been discharged from hospital and her brother's arriving tomorrow. Then I can return to the peace and space of my own bed.' She scrutinised Zoe. 'How are you doing? Did the police speak to you down at the pond?' She rubbed Rebus' ears and joined Zoe at the wooden table.

'Yeah. It was some new sergeant. Dad's on his way back from another crime scene.'

'Did they confirm the dead man is Lloyd?'

'The sergeant didn't want to. You know what they're like, always cagey, but I said I knew who it was. She nodded and asked me not to say anything as they've got to notify his relatives.'

'You know, I was thinking earlier. The amount of people who've got it in for him, they're not going to be short of suspects, are they? I don't envy them one bit. Thank goodness we don't know anyone involved this time. I'm very glad not to be investigating.'

'It's their job, Mum. Not like us amateurs.'

One of the kittens was already halfway across the kitchen floor.

'I've got twenty minutes to go before I wash this off.' Sylvia shuffled over and joined them, still in her dressing gown and slippers. She had hair dye on her roots. 'How do I get Lexi to set a timer?' she asked Zoe.

'It's Alexa, Gran.' Zoe issued the instruction to the smart speaker.

'Thank you.' Sylvia caught sight of the kitten. 'Which one's this?'

'Fran hasn't named them,' Ellie replied. 'She lets their new owners do that.'

'If they don't already have homes, can we have one, Mum? Please.' Zoe pulled an imploring face, her head tilted. 'Even better – two.'

'She's selling them privately, so I'll ask. Sal is after one too. At this rate I'll have found them all homes by the time Fran gets back.'

Sally was Ellie's best friend.

'Don't we have enough pets though?' Ellie added.

Before Zoe could answer, Sylvia said, 'What's this about a dead man?'

Zoe filled her grandmother in on what had happened in the hare meadow.

'What were you doing out so early?' Sylvia prodded Zoe.

'Taking photos for the village Springwatch Competition. I wanted to get one of the hares, boxing. We've got Chris Packham judging it this year, and I really want to win. First prize is one of his nature photography courses.'

Ellie turned to Sylvia. 'You might not know because it happened before you moved here. The dead man ran down the village lollipop lady in his van just over four years ago. Killed her. Joan Chapman.'

Sylvia gasped. 'Oh, my goodness. I do. Drink driving, wasn't it? Nothing annoys me more. So selfish.'

'It was an awful time for the family. He denied it to start with, but quickly changed his tune and pleaded guilty–'

'To reduce his sentence, I suppose.' Sylvia's tone was noticeably disapproving.

'Well, call me a cynic but… he was given four years.'

'And was released after two?'

'Yup. On licence.'

'I remember it,' said Zoe. 'I was in the sixth form. Joan's granddaughter was in my year. We were in double Biology when her mum came to collect her.'

'I recall there being an outcry about the sentence,' said Sylvia. 'People saying that four years wasn't enough for taking Joan's life.'

'His defence team cited various mitigating factors in court. Dave told me.'

'Tragic,' said Sylvia. 'I bet Joan's family weren't pleased when they were told Lloyd was being released.'

Sylvia was a retired social worker and, like Ellie, had been married to a detective.

'The local police notified them,' said Ellie. 'It was an automatic release so they couldn't object. He was never going to get a good reception after what he did – but this?'

'Didn't one of Joan's sons go off at Lloyd's father at the court?' asked Sylvia.

Ellie nodded. 'That was Ian, the eldest. Worse than that. He issued a threat, saying when Lloyd's released, he'd better watch out because they'll be there waiting.'

'Oh crikey.'

'He'd said the same thing a few times, I gather, so it wasn't as if the police could dismiss his words as an emotional reaction to the sentence.'

Sylvia nodded, as though she was absorbing the information. 'Have they appointed a lead detective, did the sergeant say?'

'It's Dad,' said Zoe. 'DS Carmichael was just getting things started until he arrives.'

'I don't envy him this one.'

Zoe was flicking through photos on her phone. She came to a close up shot of Lloyd in the water. She zoomed in and gasped. 'Mum, look at this. He's got some kind of wire round his neck.'

Ellie leaned over to get a good look at the image. As Zoe described, a thin, semi-rigid wire hung around Lloyd's neck, a red line above it. 'That's one mystery solved. Looks like picture wire. He's been garrotted.'

Chapter 3

It was mid-morning when the doorbell rang. Rebus barked several times and began whining.

Sylvia was unable to conceal a tut and shuffled across the lounge in her socks.

'Settling into a comfortable posture...' said the man on the recording.

Fat chance of that now.

'Feeling the movement of air on your skin and face...' he continued.

She opened the door.

'Feeling sensations of pressure, contact, energy...' the comforting voice continued from behind her. *'Noticing the connection with the ground, your seat, stool...'*

It was Dave, in a grey suit and a long, brown coat. 'What on earth is that?' His face was like thunder. 'Ugh...' He coughed. 'That smell.'

Rebus squealed in excitement and lunged at Dave.

'Oh, hi.' Sylvia stepped back for him to enter, shutting the door to keep the kittens safe. 'We're doing a guided mindfulness of breathing. Zoe suggested it. Do you want to join us?'

'Connecting with the sacrum, pelvis, the lumbar spine...' the recording continued.

'The mindfulness of what?' He took in her elasticated tracksuit bottoms and t-shirt; the incense burning on a dish, smoke wafting across the room.

In the lounge, Zoe and her boyfriend Finn were sitting cross-legged on the sofa, backs upright, eyes closed.

'Shifting your awareness to your breathing now,' the man said. *'In and out. Observing your body as it breathes. The breathing body.'*

'It's meditation. Be good for your blood pressure by the look of it.'

'I'm sorry but... the *breathing body*?' Dave's eyebrows had shot up and he was shaking his head.

'I imagine you're here to see Zoe?'

'Yes, apologies for barging in. I've just got back. I'm afraid I need to ask her some questions about the hare meadow.'

'Beginning to count after the out-breath...'

'I've got most of the information I need from DS Carmichael but would like to check a couple of things.'

'She's got an Air BnB changeover at 1pm and–' She caught Dave's expression.

He was looking down at his feet where a kitten was waddling away from a puddle. 'I wondered what that warm sensation was. Little monkey's peed on my shoe.'

Ten minutes later, Dave was installed at the kitchen table, a pair of Finn's white trainers poking out from the legs of his suit trousers. His suede brogue had been wiped and was drying on top of a radiator.

'Did you see anyone while you were in the hare meadow?' he asked Zoe.

'No.'

'What about on the way there? Think carefully. Did you see or meet anyone?'

'I saw quite a few people. Sally was walking Luna. She was just setting off from the house. I didn't stop as I wanted to get the best pictures and not miss the light.'

'Uh-huh.'

'I waved to the woman in the white house on the lane, just before you get to the hare meadow,' she continued. 'She was opening her curtains.'

'Who else?'

'Charlie Matthews was out for a run with Finn. They were going into Appledown Woods. Gary Piggott, the builder, was loading turf onto his pickup at the garden centre. With a young lad.'

Dave was jotting notes. 'What time was that?'

'About 6.45am. I was going to cut through the woods to get to the meadow and the pond.'

'Did you recognise the lad?'

'Not by name. I've seen him around the village.'

'What alerted you to the body in the pond?'

'I was tracking the movements of the hares across the meadow. The sun was out and it was misty. The grass was covered in dew. It looked really pretty, and I wanted to see if I could catch the hares boxing.'

'Right.'

'I was crouching, so I could keep my camera still and not disturb the hares. And so I could get some shots from ground level. There were a few ducks on the pond. One of them came up to the surface with a flourish. The movement and sound of the water caught my attention. That was when I saw him.'

'Can you describe exactly what you saw?'

'A body on its back; feet, belly and face poking slightly out of the water.'

'You didn't see anyone leaving the area, or hanging around?'

'Nope. Do you know how long he'd been in the water?'

'I can't divulge that, I'm afraid.'

Dave's phone vibrated. He accepted the call, shifting in his seat as he spoke. 'Guv?'

Sylvia gave Zoe a smile. They couldn't hear what the person was saying but could see Dave was listening intently.

'Now? Couldn't it wait 'til I've–' Dave turned to face them, his face draining of colour. 'You're kidding?'

Sylvia frowned.

'OK. I'll come in.' He rang off, then met his mum's worried gaze.

'What's happened?'

'I can't quite believe it.' His face was white. 'The chief superintendent's taken me off the case.'

'What? Why?' Sylvia knew it must be something serious for the chief super to have made the phone call.

Dave's brow was knotted. 'Conflict of interests, apparently.'

Chapter 4

Dave had gone and Sylvia was Googling 'top-feeder for beehive' on Ellie's laptop. Four months earlier she'd set up a small bee colony in the garden at the windmill, encouraged by one of their friends in the village, Sarge. Sarge and his nephew had been helping them with the garden, and the Blix family had semi-adopted the older man.

Finn charged through the door, breaking her concentration and bringing with him a waft of cool spring air.

'Kittens,' she said.

It was their password now, so everyone knew to keep them secure.

'Thanks.' He closed the door, let Rebus off the lead, and deposited his keys and phone on the kitchen table. 'I'm leaving Reeby here. Bob and I are meeting to put the flags and the markers in, for the Egg Hunt on Easter Sunday.'

'Righto.'

'It's all happening in the hare meadow. The police have put up a forensics tent and there's a team of divers searching the pond.'

'That's routine when they find a body in water. They'll be looking for a weapon, clothing, anything that might link them to the perpetrator.'

'I saw Katie Douglas. Smirking like the cat that got the cream.' He walked over to a coffee table, where a kitten was trying to climb on top of the lampshade.

Sylvia groaned. 'She's probably bribed one of the crime scene guards or tricked an officer into giving her a scoop. We know why the local paper keeps her on, but I wish she'd go and work at one of the trashy tabloids.' She found it hard to keep the disdain from her voice.

Finn picked up the kitten and rested it on his chest. 'There was a national reporter there too. ITV, I think.'

'Really?'

'She was doing a segment on Lloyd's murder. Apparently, he was released from Bronzewell Prison in Sussex. His girlfriend stood by him while he was inside. They've been together for years. Engaged. And – this is really weird, right – they were due to get married today.'

Sylvia stared at him. She was a generation older than Lloyd while Finn was a generation younger. Neither knew much about the dead man.

'Here in the village, at St Mary's.'

'Crikey. They kept that quiet. Perhaps they wanted to avoid publicity. Hecklers at the church. What else did the reporter say?'

'His fiancée is Amy Hardcastle. She works at the vet's in the village. The reporter was talking about how upsetting Lloyd's death was for her. It'll probably be on the news already. She was doing a live broadcast.'

'Ellie will know Amy. The whole thing is bizarre and unsettling. Lloyd's released from prison, after knocking down and killing the village lollipop lady, and was due to get married but someone bumps him off.' Sylvia's brain was bursting with questions.

'I was walking Rebus and pretended he was sniffing something,' Finn continued, 'but the reporter caught me listening in and gave me a dirty look.'

'Given they were getting married at St Mary's, Leonard will have got to know the couple.'

Leonard was the local vicar, a close friend of Sylvia's.

'Was meant to be at midday.'

'I'll switch on. See what they're saying.' She got up, fetched the remote control and put the TV on in the kitchen.

'... bring you a reminder of some news we covered earlier,' said a shiny-haired presenter in a brightly lit TV studio.

'Damn. We must've missed the live broadcast from the hare meadow,' Sylvia said.

'They'll repeat it,' said Finn.

'Police have issued a warrant for a male from Dover who has recently been released from prison on parole.'

'Who's this then?' asked Finn.

'Forty-two-year-old Brendan Murphy, who sometimes goes by the names Barry Connell and Bryan Cornwell, has breached his parole conditions. Despite satisfying the parole board, officials say there is a possibility Mr Murphy could be a danger to the public.'

'Oh, golly.'

'Why've they released him then?' asked Finn.

'If the parole board decide he's fit for release, they can't keep him. All they can do is put conditions in place – as they've done.'

'The police are actively investigating Mr Murphy's whereabouts. If anyone sees him, they are advised not to approach him and to report any sightings to the police on 999.'

Chapter 5

When Ellie opened the front door of the windmill, Dave was facing her, coat collar turned up, skin taut and ashen over his cheeks.

'It's not just a conflict of interests.' His voice was a whisper. 'I'm a suspect. I'm an *actual suspect.*'

'You're kidding?' She waved him in. Sylvia had told her about the chief super's call. 'On what basis?' She was drying her hands on a tea towel.

'They have evidence that incriminates me.' She caught the flatness in his voice. 'And they're searching my flat.'

Ellie gulped. This was serious.

'They'll only get a warrant, so I consented to the search. Best to get it over with.'

'What are they looking for?'

'Don't know.' He closed his eyes and gently shook his head, as though the idea was too awful to imagine. 'Anything that confirms their suspicions, I imagine.'

'Have you got an alibi?'

'No. The crime scene pathologist has estimated the time of death as between 3am and 5am. I was at home on my own. Had an early night and left at 6am. Was called out to a crime scene in Kingsdown.'

'What's the super said?'

'He's told me to go on leave until the case is solved. And to stay in the area in case they have further questions.'

Dave hung up his coat and joined Ellie at the kitchen table, pacing up and down and raking his hand through his hair. 'All the neighbours will see the police vehicles at my place.' He groaned and covered his face with his hands. 'They'll think I've done something wrong. The village gossip is going to be off the scale.'

On the table, a kitten was having a one-sided boxing match with Ellie's weeping fig plant.

Dave's face softened. 'My shoe hasn't recovered.' He forced a chuckle. 'It pongs. And it's got a stain all over the front.'

Ellie tried not to laugh, relieved for a bit of humour. She was worried about the evidence Dave mentioned. 'I can offer you a cup of tea or something stronger. There's some wine in the fridge from last night.'

'Tea, please. It's only 4pm. Might take you up on the alcohol in a bit. Seeing as I'm off-duty *indefinitely* now.' He began pacing again.

Despite his attempt at a joke, Ellie caught the pain in his last sentence; his agitation.

'They'll have the case solved quickly, I'm sure. Things will be back to normal then.' She wasn't as certain as she sounded but she wanted to support Dave, help him feel positive. It wasn't that she thought he was guilty. It was the mention of... 'What sort of evidence do they think they have?' She hoped her voice didn't sound too on edge.

He sat down. 'A witness has testified that I've been threatening Lloyd.'

The kitten abandoned the plant and waddled over to Dave, tail bolt upright.

'You haven't, right?' His response was a shock. Ellie didn't know what she'd been expecting but it certainly wasn't this.

'Of *course* not.' Dave picked up the tiny bundle of fur. 'Hello, buddy. Was it you who peed on my shoe? Or one of your siblings?'

He turned back to Ellie. 'I haven't had anything to do with him since I gave evidence at his trial. Unfortunately, the witness has said they have text messages between them and Lloyd referring to my alleged threats.'

Ellie frowned. 'That doesn't prove anything except that *that's* what they claim. Your colleagues will know that. They'll bear it in mind as they go through all the comms data and social media. Who's the witness?' She was struggling to get her head round the idea of Dave threatening anyone. It wasn't how she saw him at all.

'The super hasn't told me. Now I'm a suspect I'm not even allowed to go into my work email.'

It made sense, and Dave would know this too; but Ellie could see how it might feel he was being excluded from something that was usually his domain.

The kitten was now on its back, paws massaging the air and purring quietly.

'It's so embarrassing.' Dave gently rested his head on the kitten's soft belly. 'My whole career, I've never had anything like this happen. I've worked my socks off, focused on the job, the community. Kept my nose clean.' He sat back up and looked at her, his troubled eyes searching hers. 'What am I going to do?'

'Everyone knows your reputation is impeccable. Your colleagues aren't going to believe claims unless there's solid evidence to back them up.'

Ellie got up and strode across to the window, dabbing at smears on the glass from the kittens' paws and noses.

She turned back to the table.

He had his warrant card out and was gazing at it, his expression wistful. 'All my life, I only ever wanted to follow in Dad's footsteps and be a detective. I can't believe this is happening.'

Ellie knew this was true. She remembered Dave endlessly making her, Nick and Sally play cops and robbers when they were kids. Then, how chuffed he'd been fifteen years later at his passing out parade. Face beaming, a man whose childhood dream had just come true. His detective chief inspector dad there, proudly watching him.

'Looking at things logically,' she said, as much for her own benefit as Dave's, 'whoever has said you've been threatening Lloyd has to be someone he was in close contact with, right? Someone he trusted enough to share the information with. My money would be on his dad. Arthur's staunchly defended Lloyd ever since Joan's death.'

Dave nodded. 'I had him in mind. Or Amy. She's his girlfriend.'

'You know he was meant to be getting married today, don't you?'

'Yes. I was just getting myself up to date with their relationship when I got sent home. They've kept the wedding quiet.' He glanced round the kitchen, as though lost in thought. 'It's a bit odd that he gets killed on the morning of his wedding. Is it a coincidence?'

'Maybe not. Perhaps someone didn't want him marrying her. Oh well – your colleagues will find out soon enough.'

Ellie sensed there was something else Dave wanted to say. She put the kettle on and waited for him to gather his thoughts.

He released the kitten onto the floor. 'You know, Lloyd blamed me for him going down. He vowed revenge from the very start. Before the trial. Right from when we arrested him.'

A shudder ran over Ellie. Things were getting worse by the minute. 'I didn't know that. What sort of revenge?'

It was like a dripping tap. Each time she found out more, another drop of information cranked up her unease.

'Nothing specific. "I'll get you, you so-and-so," that sort of thing. I didn't want to worry you. And it's not an uncommon thing to happen.'

Ellie frowned.

'I was the lead detective on the investigation. Perpetrators can get fixated on the person in charge.'

'Your colleagues will know about that then too. They'll bear it in mind when they're evaluating evidence. They're probably just doing due diligence, taking you off the case, searching your flat.'

As she spoke though she was aware of a pulling in her stomach. Dave was a well-respected officer and a valued team member. She had no doubt his peers and superiors would investigate thoroughly, but there was something odd about the chief superintendent weighing in. It suggested a serious cause for concern. Or – influence from higher up.

And taking him off the case was one thing, but searching his flat? That was a very different matter. The former could be about the integrity of the investigation. The latter required grounds for suspicion.

'Has Lloyd contacted you at all? Issued any threats since the time of the investigation?'

Dave shook his head.

'Not since he was released?'

'Nothing.'

'How could you have threatened him then if there's been no contact between you?'

He gave a long, slow shrug, eyes wide. 'I don't understand it either. I'm baffled.'

'It's a bit strange that he was the one threatening you, yet he alleged *you've* threatened him.'

'Quite.'

'It doesn't make sense. And what motive would you have for wanting to harm him?'

He shook his head, his mouth curled in perplexity.

'It's ridiculous. It's not as if you're a new recruit. You've built up your reputation over a two-decade career. You'll be going for chief inspector next. As if you'd jeopardise all that for a nobody like him. You've got so much to lose.'

Outside in the drive, car doors slammed. Voices. Shoes on the path. A rap on the door.

It was two detectives, one female, the other, tall, male, with a gingery beard. Two uniformed officers stood behind them.

Ellie guessed the female was the sergeant who had questioned Zoe at the crime scene, DS Carmichael.

'Mrs Blix,' she said as she entered the windmill and introduced herself with a strong country accent.

'What's going on?' Ellie looked from the detective to Dave, who had swung his legs round to face his colleagues.

'Guv,' she said nervously to Dave. 'You weren't at home so we guessed you'd be here.' She showed her warrant card, presumably for procedure, her hand shaking slightly. 'Dave Blix, I am arresting you on suspicion of murdering Lloyd Durden.'

'What?' Ellie was shaking too. 'How come?' Hadn't Dave said he hadn't seen Lloyd? The police must've discovered something new.

'I haven't done anything,' said Dave, as he looked pleadingly at Ellie.

Ellie caught the tremble in his voice, the bewildered expression in his eyes.

'You do not have to say anything but anything you do say will be taken down in evidence and–'

Dave spoke quietly but more determinedly now. 'I've done nothing wrong. Ells, you guys know what to do, right?'

Chapter 6

'Arrested?' Zoe's eyes widened in alarm.

Dave had just left. The three women sat round the kitchen table, as they did every day. Sipping a drink, talking, admiring the glorious yellow of the daffodils which Sylvia had picked in the garden.

Except – today things were different. The news was on low on the kitchen TV and a heavy atmosphere lay in the room.

Zoe picked at the purple varnish on her fingernails.

'Couldn't you use some remover if you want to get rid of it?' said Sylvia. 'Instead of flicking it all over the table.'

'I'm not *flicking* it.' Zoe gave her gran a sideways glance.

They were all tense.

Ellie had caught herself snapping at a customer who was complaining a little earlier.

She filled them in. The threat claims. The messages the police had got hold of. The search. Dave's comment about 'knowing what to do'.

'By that, do we suppose he wants us to investigate?' asked Sylvia.

Ellie shrugged. 'I'm assuming so. There aren't too many options. I didn't attempt to clarify in front of the police because, if we're going to investigate, Dave might not want them knowing.'

'Duh, Mum. He's been arrested on suspicion of a murder. What help would he need right now?' Zoe looked from her gran to her mother, her cheeks flushed. 'He hardly would've meant, could you pick up his dry cleaning or water his pot plants? He knows we investigate crimes for people. That *must* be what he meant, surely? We've got to help him. He's relying on us.'

'Of course. I just didn't want to make the wrong assumption.'

'I agree with Zoe,' Sylvia added. 'He must've meant that.'

'How long will he be at the police station?' asked Zoe.

Ellie let Sylvia answer.

'Twenty-four hours and then they either have to charge him or apply for an extension. They're searching his flat, so it'll depend on what they find.' She paused. 'Evidence can, of course, be interpreted in a number of ways.' She looked at Ellie nervously, and Ellie wondered what Sylvia was making of this development. Dave was her son, after all.

'*Gran.*' Zoe's tone was remonstrative and her nostrils were flaring. 'This is Dad we're talking about. They're not going to find anything. It's got to be a mistake. Dad wouldn't murder anyone.'

'Oh, I'm sure you're right, but we might as well be practical about this.'

Ellie tuned into Sylvia's intonation. She heard doubt. And genuine worry.

Sylvia faced Ellie. 'You and I both know they won't have arrested him without good reason.' She spoke softly, as though wanting to quell her own anxiety. 'They're either pretty sure about the threats or–'

'Maybe there's something we don't know yet,' Zoe suggested.

Ellie and Sylvia caught each other's eye.

'Some police technicality. That's always happening on TrueCrimeTV.'

Ellie could see Zoe was upset about her dad, but things didn't add up. 'I was wondering if they've found further evidence.' She was thinking aloud. It was *always* about evidence. 'To start with, he was simply removed from the case for conflict of interest. If they had enough evidence to arrest him, they'd have done it then, surely?'

'I would imagine so,' Sylvia replied. 'He'll get legal advice from a solicitor at least.'

'I can't believe the two of you are being so laid back about this.' Zoe stood up, her chair screeching on the hard floor as she pushed it back. 'Dad's been arrested and you're both sitting here, calm as anything, saying, "Oh well, he'll get legal advice". What if they charge him? He might go to *prison*.' She emphasised the last word, eyes filling with tears.

Ellie took a deep breath. Zoe adored her dad. It was inevitable she was going to be upset – and panic.

The TV broadcast caught Ellie's attention. They'd put it on for updates.

'Police are appealing for witnesses following the death of a Kent man. Emergency services were on the scene in Lower

Wootton, near Deal, at seven o'clock this morning, following reports of a dead body in the pond in what locals call Hare Meadow.'

'Turn it up, Zo,' said Ellie. 'The remote's by you.'

'The man has been identified as Lloyd Durden, who was recently released from prison. The police are looking to trace Mr Durden's last known movements. They would like to speak to anyone who saw Mr Durden on Friday evening, or during the night and early hours of Saturday morning.'

The three of them stared at the screen, rapt.

'The police would also like to hear from anyone with CCTV or dashcam footage of Mr Durden. Please get in touch quoting reference number...'

'It's good that it's on the news,' said Ellie. 'Hopefully, they'll get lots of leads.'

'And minimal crank calls and time wasters,' muttered Sylvia. 'Changing the subject, do you know Amy Hardcastle?' she asked Ellie.

'Yes. I know Amy. She was in our year at school. Lloyd was a couple of years older than her. They were together for donkeys' years.' A memory tapped at Ellie. 'I'll check with Sally. I'm pretty sure Amy was part of the Wootton panto group. The main thing I remember is Amy's always adored animals.' She stopped. 'Right. Let's get mugs of tea and start compiling a list of who might have had it in for Lloyd.'

'I made a fresh batch of hot cross buns last night,' Sylvia told them. 'With apple and cinnamon. We can have one of them each with butter. Would you like that, Zo?'

Zoe shot her grandmother a dirty look. 'I'm not six, you know. I don't want a flippin' hot cross bun. I want Dad here. Safe.'

Ellie slid her arm round Zoe's waist. 'I'm definitely up for a bun,' she said to Sylvia. 'I was here last night when you had them in the oven. They smelled delicious.' She turned to Zoe, speaking gently. 'Don't worry about your dad, lovey. Between the police, his solicitor and us, we'll soon get to the bottom of this and have him home.'

Zoe yanked her mum's arm off and shuffled over to the sink where two kittens were playing with water in a mug. 'You two need to shift.' She moved them and filled the kettle.

'I'll grab my notepad from the office,' said Ellie. 'Are you going to join us, Zo? We'd really value your input.'

'Suppose,' she said sulkily. 'Can you both stop acting like everything's fine though? It's freaking me out.'

'OK,' said Ellie, as she walked. 'Point taken. I think we're just trying to... er... get the balance right between...' She stared at Sylvia, hoping she'd chip in.

Sylvia caught on. '... between trying to be positive... and accepting the seriousness of the situation.' She gave Zoe a kind smile. 'You said yourself you're worried your dad's going to prison. You also said the police must've made a mistake.'

Zoe gave a tiny nod of acknowledgement.

Sylvia carried on. 'We're all feeling our way. Doing our best. OK? No one thinks you're a child. And you're right.' Her voice took on a sad tone. 'We do need to accept that things aren't looking good for your father at the moment.'

'O-kay.' Zoe didn't sound wholly satisfied; but none of them were.

'How many kittens have we got?' said Ellie, returning with a notepad. At her feet, one was busily chewing her bootlace.

'There are a couple here.' Zoe pointed at the worktop. 'They're a bit wet but they seem to be enjoying themselves. I'll check in the lounge too. It's a bit quiet in there so they're either asleep or causing trouble.' She nipped across the room, returning quickly. 'The others are asleep on Dad's jumper on the sofa. Right, let's start this meeting.'

'OK,' said Sylvia, having swallowed a mouthful of buttered bun. 'Potential suspects for Lloyd's murder.'

'We usually start by thinking about who would gain from him not being around, don't we?' Zoe said. 'In this case, the suspect pool could potentially include everyone he's upset with Joan's death.'

'That means Joan's family,' said Ellie. 'Her son, Ian, went off at Lloyd's dad at the court. Swore revenge on Lloyd. Ian would be a good place to start. Hopefully he'll be able to fill us in on what's going on with the family. How they felt about Lloyd coming out of prison. Who was particularly upset about it?'

'I was wondering if someone wanted to stop him from marrying Amy,' said Sylvia.

'Yes. Did anyone in the Hardcastle family dislike or disapprove of him?'

'Leonard might know about that,' said Sylvia. 'He was marrying them. He'll have had conversations with them both to get to know them. I'll have a chat with him after church tomorrow. See what he knows.'

'Then there's Dave.' Ellie mentioned the lack of motive.

'Wait,' said Zoe. 'We're not seriously believing Dad's killed this Lloyd bloke, are we?' She glanced from Sylvia to Ellie.

Zoe's question stopped Ellie in her tracks. She'd been asking herself the same thing ever since Dave told her what the chief super had said.

'Huh?' Sylvia frowned. 'I thought you wanted us to acknowledge the seriousness of the situation more?'

'I did,' said Zoe. 'I *do*. But not by assuming Dad's guilty. Lloyd vowing revenge on Dad suggests *he* wanted to cause Dad harm, not the other way round.'

'Well, when you put it like that, no, I don't believe he killed Lloyd,' said Ellie. 'But my point is the police *might*.'

'Mum!'

'They don't arrest people without good reason. So, I think, in order for us to help him as much as possible, we need to believe in him while trying to counter any evidence they may have.'

'You mean accept he might be guilty.'

'That's not what I said at all. I said accept the fact the police *might* think he is. We can't sit here saying it's all hunky-dory when he's in custody under arrest.'

Zoe went back to picking her nail varnish.

'What Dave said is right,' said Sylvia. 'It *is* quite common for criminals to get fixated on the officers in charge. Ron had it on a few occasions too.'

Ron was Sylvia's late husband and Dave's father.

'Rather than take responsibility for their actions, some criminals are determined to blame someone else.' She shook her head in annoyance. 'But it doesn't follow that Dave would've wanted to harm Lloyd in return. I'll have a dig around. Lloyd was released on licence, so I'll see if I can find out who he was reporting to. Find out a bit about his state of mind before he was released.'

'While we're talking about people who didn't support Lloyd after Joan's death, as soon as it came out that Lloyd was under the influence of alcohol, his sister very publicly disowned him.' Ellie's face was serious. 'Lydia, her name is.'

'Not the Lydia who's the practice manager at the doctor's surgery?' asked Sylvia. 'Slight stutter and owns a chocolate Labrador called Barney?'

'Yes, that's her. Oh my goodness, I'd forgotten about her stutter. Lots of the kids at school used to tease her. Let's see what she can tell us. And once the police have given Amy some space, we'll need to talk to her. Sounds like she was the person who's been closest to Lloyd for a long time. I particularly want to speak to her because she's bound to know if someone has been threatening Lloyd.'

'And given she stuck by him while he was in prison, she'll know if he made any enemies while he was in there. If we have to wait a while to speak to her, we could ask his father a few questions.'

'Good thinking,' said Zoe. 'And Finn and Charlie often bump into Joan's son, Ian, in the mornings in Appledown Woods when they're running. If you're looking for a low-key time to speak to him, he's usually walking his collie there around 7am.'

'That's handy info. Thanks.'

'So, we've got Ian, Lydia, Amy, and Lloyd's dad, Arthur, to speak to,' said Zoe. 'As you went to school with Amy, Mum, do you want to chat to her?'

'Yep. Why don't you and your gran talk to Lydia and Arthur. And I'll speak to Amy and Ian? I'd really like to know what he's got to say.'

Sylvia and Zoe nodded.

'The two key things we need to establish are,' Ellie continued, 'number one, who saw Lloyd last? Two, where was everyone between 3am and 5am?'

Zoe was jiggling her leg. ‘Do you think the police will release Dad this evening?’

This was on Ellie’s mind too. She hated the thought of Dave spending a night in the cells; cold, uncomfortable and worried about his future.

Chapter 7

It was dark when Ellie returned to the pet shop, and the staff had locked up and gone home. Her pet-sitting duties were primarily about the kittens as they weren't being sold through the shop. Thankfully, she was only required to sleep at the shop each night for security, not check on the animals. There was no way she was going to walk round in the dark with pet snakes and rats. Fran had asked the staff to do that.

Ellie took Tabitha and the kittens in through the flat door and upstairs. The lights were on and so was the heating, and a waft of perfume hit Ellie. Definitely not how Ellie had left it. Sophie, the owner's daughter, had a flat in Sandwich but often used her old bedroom. Looked like she was either in, or had been. There was, however, no thumping music so Ellie suspected the latter.

'Sophie?'

No answer.

Sophie and Zoe were the same age, childhood friends, and Zoe had alluded to a night out earlier, over supper. Clubbing in Canterbury. Perhaps that was where Sophie had gone.

Ellie took the carry basket into the kitchen, shut the door and let the kittens and their mum find the litter tray. She re-filled the water bowl and put down fresh food. Fran had said for Ellie to keep them in the spare bedroom with her at night, and either leave them there with a litter tray or bring them into whichever room she was in.

After the day's events, Ellie was longing for a soak in the bath. She was worried about Dave and wanted to have a mull over what they'd learnt. Before she left the windmill, she hadn't been able to get in the bathroom because Zoe was in there with a friend, applying fake tan.

Ellie made a cup of herbal tea and took the kittens back into the spare room. She left the door open, closed all the other bedroom doors, and the doors into the kitchen and lounge.

Phew.

She deposited her phone on the bathroom cabinet.

Soon the bath was full. She lit a candle and climbed in, stirring the delicious bubbles and inhaling the lavender and geranium aromas.

Tabitha stole in and jumped up onto the cabinet housing the handbasin, presumably seeking a bit of time-out from her youngsters. She crouched down, curled her pretty tail round her feet and began to doze contentedly.

Ellie had been in the bath for all of five minutes when her phone rang. Could it be Dave, calling from the custody suite at the police station? Or Sylvia with news about Lloyd?

She climbed out of the bath and reached for the phone, swiping the 'accept call' button just as it rang off.

'Darn. Typical.' She checked her call log. It was a local landline number, not one in her phonebook. She was about to return the call when it rang again. Same number.

'Hello? Ellie Blix speaking.'

'Oh, hello Mrs Blix. Sorry to disturb you.' It was a woman's voice. 'I'm ringing from the house behind the shop. At the end of the garden. Fran said you were staying.'

Images of calamities were pouring into Ellie's mind as she tried to figure out why the woman was ringing. Had she blocked their drive at some point? Scraped their car? Or committed some other neighbourly sin?

'My husband says Houdini is in our garden.'

'Sorry, who's Houdini?' She wasn't sure whether to be amused or annoyed. Fran hadn't mentioned any other animals.

'Sophie's white rabbit. My husband's out there now, trying to catch him.'

'Oh, crikey. I was in the bath. I'll get dressed and come round. You're on The Ridge, aren't you?'

'Yes. We're 478. Long Meadow. Austrian chalet-type house.' She hesitated. 'Sophie was home earlier. I'm not sure she always... er... closes the hutch properly.' Her voice softened. 'He often seems to... um... *get out* when she's home.'

'Well, let's get him back before he disappears for good. I'll be round in a couple of minutes. I just need to get the kittens back into the spare room, otherwise they'll be disappearing too.'

Ellie was beginning to regret allowing Fran to talk her into pet- sitting. If it hadn't been for the urgent hip surgery, she wouldn't have given in.

Ten minutes later, Ellie was in the back garden at Long Meadow, in the dark, crawling round the grass on her hands and knees with the woman who'd rung her, trying to persuade Houdini the rabbit to stop lolloping off.

'He went that way,' said Jim, who seemed to have designated himself the operational chief. In brown corduroy trousers and a cream cardigan, he was pointing towards the summer house with one hand and holding a pipe in the other.

Ellie got up. After nearly twenty years of running a cleaning business, her knees were not up to this. She followed Carol 'that way' on foot, only for Jim to announce that Houdini had now gone in the other direction.

After a few minutes of going back and forth, and failing to persuade the rabbit to curtail his adventures, Carol got to her feet too. Like Ellie, she had wet patches on the knees of her trousers. 'That's it. I've had enough.'

Ellie's thoughts entirely.

'Perhaps you would like to get down there, darling, and have a go? I'm going to wash my hands and change out of these soaking wet trousers.'

Ellie stayed silent, wondering how many times this scenario had played out before. They must dread Sophie coming home.

'There he is,' Carol shouted, as Houdini's white bottom bobbed towards the house and a rather lovely fishpond.

'Nope, gone again,' Jim muttered, and sucked on his pipe. 'Little blighter.'

'Got him,' shouted Carol. 'He's in here.' She slammed the French windows shut and beckoned them in with an exuberant wave. She scooped up the rabbit before he had a chance to make off again.

'Hold onto him, please,' said Ellie jubilantly. 'He is going straight back into his cage and I'm going to check the latch. And put a padlock on it if I have to.'

Five minutes later, the three of them were in the kitchen diner with Houdini the rabbit.

'How many times has this happened then?' Ellie couldn't resist asking them.

Carol rolled her eyes. 'Goodness knows. It's a regular occurrence. Sophie is a lovely girl but not great on responsibility.'

'She went out the night before you arrived,' Jim added. 'Left the lights on and the kitchen window open, didn't she? Got home around 4am. She woke up another neighbour's dog – and me.'

'Was it definitely her?' asked Carol.

He nodded. 'Since I was awake, I got up to check it was Fran's place. Saw the lights go off.' His face was full of concern. 'According to the news, Lloyd Durden was killed in the early hours of Saturday morning. Sophie needs to be careful, coming back from these clubs. Walking about in the dark when these dangerous men are about. Anything could happen.'

Chapter 8 SUNDAY

Sylvia had not long got off to sleep when she was woken by barks. Downstairs, Rebus was going crazy at the door. With any luck Zoe or Finn would get up and see what was going on.

Then she remembered Zoe had gone clubbing and Finn had gone back to his house. She'd have to get up and see what the commotion was.

She pulled on her dressing gown and slippers and hurried to the front door amid a frenzy of raps.

'Ellie?'

It was Dave's voice. He must've just been released from custody.

He rapped on the door again.

'Ellie. It's me. Are you there?'

As soon as Sylvia opened the door, Rebus hurled himself at Dave, squealing and writhing.

'She's at the pet shop with the kittens. What time is it?'

'Oh, of course. It's just after 1am.' He looked awful. Collar turned up. Stubbly chin. Bed-head hair and red eyes.

'Come in.' She stood back, ushering him in. 'What did the police have to say?' She was hoping he'd been released with no further action.

He was shaking his head, crestfallen. 'They've released me under investigation.'

Sylvia bit her lip. That meant they weren't convinced he was innocent.

'I've got to stay in the village and can't go back to my flat yet.'

Sylvia shut the door, a swirl of emotions coursing through her. 'Well, thank goodness they've released you at least.'

'They've found further incriminating evidence. Blood on my trainers under the stairs at my flat.'

'Blood?' Sylvia's head spun slightly as she said the word. 'Whose blood?'

'Not a clue. They're waiting for the test results from the lab.' He took two steps in one direction, then two back.

Sylvia stared at him, barely able to take in what he'd just said.

'And they've found my shoe treads at the pond. From the trainers.'

That was a shock. 'How come? Were you there?'

'No. I wasn't. I don't understand how any of this evidence has turned up.' He threw his hands in the air. 'I'm a detective inspector, for goodness' sake. And all the while they're investigating me, the real killer is still about.'

Sylvia was still processing what Dave was saying.

'Plus – they've found picture wire and cutters in the cupboard under my kitchen sink.'

'Is the wire yours?'

'No. I don't use it. Everything of mine has a hook. I stopped using wire yonks ago when it gave way, and a mirror came crashing down.' He sighed. 'Anyway, the point is – that's enough evidence to charge me, Mum. The picture wire. My trainer treads and the blood.'

Sylvia's hand went out to steady herself. Dave was right. The situation was looking very serious. They had to help him challenge the evidence.

'Is the blood likely to be Lloyd's? I can't really take this in.'

'I've no idea whose it is. I run in those trainers so maybe I hurt my foot. Burst a blister or scratched a leg on brambles.'

'You'd have known though, surely?' Sylvia was thinking about the meadow. 'Have you been in the area by the pond with those shoes on recently?'

'Not for a couple of weeks. I twisted my ankle in the woods and haven't been running. Foot went down a rabbit hole and I was over.' He was tapping at keys on his phone.

'Well, how have your shoe prints got by the pond? And picture wire in your flat?'

'The only explanation I can think of is that someone's trying to frame me. Maybe they've been in my flat. I'm hoping my home CCTV will show if someone's got in.' He tutted and placed his phone down. 'Unfortunately, I can't access it. I've tried doing it on my phone but it's not working for some reason.'

Sylvia filled the kettle and flicked it on to boil. Her body was shaking and she felt sick. 'Maybe the police have switched the security system off? To get in or to analyse it – or both.'

Dave shrugged.

'When was the last time you wore those trainers?'

'When I twisted my ankle. That would've been two weeks tomorrow. I don't go in that cupboard often. It's where I keep the hoover and some coats. Shoes. Wellies and boots. The cleaner would be more likely to know if they went missing.'

Blix Blitz did Dave's cleaning, Ellie's company.

'I can check our records and find out who last cleaned your place. See if they remember seeing them.' She popped teabags in their mugs and poured cold milk on top.

'Mum!'

'What? Oh, damn. My mind's all over the place.' She decanted the milk into another mug and used boiling water this time. 'It might be worth compiling a list of everyone who's been in your flat in the last few weeks.'

'Yeah. The solicitor said the same. I've started that. The custody sergeant took my phone.'

'Are the shoe treads definitely yours?'

'They're waiting on confirmatory results from the lab. Eyeball tests suggest they're mine. They'll have taken soil samples too.' He raked his hands through his hair. 'I need a drink.'

'Are you their prime suspect?'

'I don't know. They're keeping their cards close to their chests.'

Sylvia's head was still spinning. 'You know what? Stuff tea. I need something a bit more fortifying.'

'I was about to ask if my whisky is still here from Christmas. Is it OK to check?'

'Sure. If you know where it was. Although Finn and his friends might have polished it off.'

He strode into the lounge.

Sylvia sat down at the kitchen table, willing her brain to start computing. To come up with a rational explanation for why her son's trainer treads were at the crime scene. And why they had blood on them.

Dave returned with a half-drunk bottle of brown liquid. 'Someone's had the Glenfiddich. Replaced it with a cheap bottle of Tesco's own.' He held up the bottle and went to a cupboard for tumblers. 'Would you like some?'

'Please.' She watched him pour. The police would have asked for some of the forensics to be fast-tracked. Hopefully, that would include Dave's trainer sole and the blood. 'How reliable are shoe treads?'

'It's extremely serious.' His face was downcast. 'In conjunction with soil analysis, and biological analyses from the shoe wearer – very. They're one of the foundations of most murder trials.'

Chapter 9

Sylvia re-filled her hot water bottle and left Dave on the couch with a sleeping bag and Rebus. Went back upstairs. There was no sign of Zoe. It was possible she'd gone to Finn's, rather than come home in the small hours and wake her up, but Sylvia was too tired to worry. Zoe was an adult now.

She climbed into bed with her thoughts jangling. It was worrying enough Dave being arrested for murder, but this new evidence made her feel distinctly uneasy. The tread was bad enough... but blood on the very same trainer? And the picture wire?

Dave denied knowing anything about any of it, so there weren't too many options. Either someone was trying to get him into trouble, or someone was using him. Or –

which she refused to accept – there was something he wasn't telling them.

Surely not?

He was her son.

What was it Ron used to say?

'Murder detectives are like heads over the parapet. Sooner or later, someone comes for you.'

If it hadn't happened to Dave yet, maybe now was his time.

She rubbed her stomach and wondered whether there were any antacids in the bathroom cabinet.

When Ellie got back, they'd have a good talk to Dave.

But much as she wanted to believe him, her thoughts kept circling back to her own questions from earlier. The footprints, the blood, the wire.

She knew the police would be checking all these factors, but they had no way of knowing what the investigating team had found because Dave had been removed from all comms. And that meant Blix Investigators had to come up with alternative explanations.

Instead of relaxing into sleep, her mind kept throwing up more ideas and questions. The possibilities were endless and depressing. But did she really think Dave was capable of murder?

No way.

This was *Dave*. Her son. She'd carried him in her womb; given birth to him. He'd always been a good cop, hadn't he? Like his dad. This was the sort of mad thinking that occurred at silly o'clock.

But this wasn't the only aspect that was bothering her. Dave and Ellie loved each other. And now he'd decided not to take the promotion in Birmingham, there was finally the chance they might get back together. OK, it wasn't urgent but it was still important. Was this going to be ruined too? The thing they'd all been hoping for, for the last two years?

The hours rolled by.

3am became 4am and she was too hot, so she lobbed the hot water bottle on the floor. Around 4am, she'd just dropped off when Rebus sneaked into her room, climbed on the bed and woke her up. At 5am, she got up and went downstairs to the office, trying not to wake Dave on the sofa. She ushered Rebus in, shut the door and switched the light on.

Ellie's desktop computer took a few minutes to start up, but she was soon in the Blix Blitz customer management system. She looked up Dave's records. He had weekly cleans on a Wednesday. She pulled a Post-it off the pack and made a note of the names of the cleaners from the last four weeks. All Ellie's regular staff.

She was about to log off when she saw a note on the file saying that the regular cleaner had been off sick, and Ellie had got an agency person in. Name of Emily. She added the name to the Post-it. She'd ask Ellie about her in the morning, if she ever got any sleep.

Fortunately, when she got back into bed, she dropped off straightaway and the next she knew, it was nearly six o'clock. The sun was coming up and Rebus was scratching at the door, wondering where Ellie was; no doubt wanting to go out in the garden and have his kibble.

Her temples throbbed from lack of sleep; her body ached with exhaustion. It was going to be a long day.

Rebus jumped on the bed and began his usual effusive licking.

'Enough. Off,' she said grumpily. 'C'mon. Let's let you out. Mummy will be back soon. You can lick her.'

In the lounge, Dave hadn't stirred, so she let Rebus out and switched the kettle on. While it was boiling, she texted Ellie, saying Dave had been released pending further investigation and was at the windmill.

Her phone dinged with Ellie's reply.

'Won't be long. Will drop the kittens off then I'm going for a dog walk with Sally. Hoping to find Ian.'

She started texting a reply, telling her about the new evidence against Dave but clicked the app shut.

She'd let Ellie enjoy her walk. Dave could fill her in when she got back. And Zoe, whenever she got home.

She made a coffee and went back into the office. Sat in Ellie's chair and closed her eyes briefly, wondering how on earth she was going to get through the day on almost no sleep. What she needed was a change of focus. Something cheery.

She opened the Lower Wootton Facebook page, to check the timings of events on Good Friday and Easter Sunday. Scrolled for a bit. Past a post about the Hot Cross Bun challenge. The Bunny Hop Egg Hunt. The Easter Parade. Morris Dancing.

Then, on *The Wootton Gazette*'s page, a picture of Dave flashed up, standing in front of a marked police car. Her heart sank as she read the headline: LOCAL LOTHARIO ARRESTED FOR MURDER.

Chapter 10

Appledown Woods were a sea of green and brown in the spring. It was too early for bluebells. A few clumps of daffodils lingered where there was shade, interspersed with the dense carpet of green. Wood anemones wove through the grass, straining their necks and tilting towards the sun.

Ellie and Sally had Rebus and Luna off the lead. The two dogs lolloped along the chalky path, snuffling in the undergrowth and bushes, chasing each other happily. Friends since they were puppies, they loved nothing more than a run in the woods.

The dogs playing together gave Ellie the chance to air her ideas with her best friend and to get her perspective. The kittens were settled in the office at the windmill, and she'd checked the Blix Blitz diary. She could relax for an hour.

'I can't say that Dave being arrested for murder was on my list of likely events at Easter,' said Ellie, as she strode along the path.

'The cops have released him though, so they're obviously reasonably happy with what he's said.'

With all the rabbit drama, Ellie hadn't checked her phone until that morning. She'd got Sylvia's text then, saying Dave was at the windmill. When she got home from the pet shop, she'd had a quick chat with him, grabbed her wellies and Rebus, and headed out to meet Sally.

'Yes, but *pending further investigation*. I intend probing him further when I get back home. Something doesn't add up.' She told Sally about the article in the local newspaper. 'Sylvia saw it.'

Sally groaned. 'Katie Flippin' Douglas strikes again. I swear that woman must chomp wasps for breakfast. How's Dave taking it?'

'He's broken. Honestly. I haven't seen him as down since his dad died. When I got home, he had his head in his hands. He's spent years building his reputation and he's proud of it. Justifiably too. Now, every man and his dog are going to be thinking he's killed Lloyd Durden.' She kicked a stone.

'Someone needs to sue that woman for defamation,' said Sally. 'The amount of hack jobs she's run on people in the village.'

'We've known for a while now the newspaper has a contact who leaks police information. That's infuriating enough. Thing is, Katie knows enough to stay within a hair's breadth of the truth so no-one can go after her. Dave *has* been arrested so it's not defamation.'

'What's he saying about the evidence then?'

'That it's extremely serious but is adamant he knows nothing about any of it.'

'Meaning what? That someone's been in his flat?'

'I guess.'

'How can they have got in? He's got fancy security at his place. I dropped off Pete's electric saw a while back, for Dave's logs, and managed to set off his burglar alarm.'

'Yeah. An alarm and CCTV. He's succeeded – finally this morning – in getting into the security system server on my laptop, but there are gaps where the CCTV hasn't recorded.'

'How would that happen?'

'He's not sure. Either it was turned off or there was some kind of system failure or outage.'

Sally pondered this. 'What happens when there's a power cut?'

This was why Ellie liked problem solving with her.

'I asked that too. It's got battery back-up.'

'Thing is, Ells, he works shifts and is out of the house for long stretches. It wouldn't be hard for someone to plot his movements and suss out when it was safe to break in. It would take someone with pretty sophisticated electronic knowledge though. They'd need to switch the alarm off and the CCTV.'

'It all feels so alien. I mean, we have burglaries here in the village, and the occasional murder, but the break-ins are usually pretty low-tech, aren't they?'

'Oh, I don't know,' Sally said. 'Quite a few of the big houses have alarm systems. Don't you remember the spate of robberies in the gated community over at Hawkshill? It was a gang from Ashford. They managed to switch the alarms and CCTV off. Turned out the guy that did their tech stuff used to work for an alarm company in London.'

'I'm sure the police will find out what's happened. It's just the timescale. Dave is worried sick. His job's so important to him.'

Sally nodded.

'He'll hate the thought of people thinking either he's killed someone or is involved with *any* sort of crime.'

They walked on.

'Anyway,' Ellie said. 'Let's change the subject. What do you remember about Lydia Durden from school? And Amy Hardcastle.'

'Lydia's the practice manager at the doctor's surgery?'

'Yes.'

'She had a crush on Dave at school. They were partnered on that Geography field trip on Hambrook Marshes. Do you remember?'

'When she fell in the Stour? Oh, my goodness, that's right. And Dave waded in and pulled her out.'

'After that, he was her hero. She hung round after him, hoping he'd notice her romantically. But he never did as he was busy trying to persuade you to go out with him.' Sally chuckled.

'How long ago those days seem now,' said Ellie wistfully. 'Someone falling in the river was the most serious thing we had to worry about. Life seems so much more complicated these days.'

'I agree. Pete and I were discussing Lloyd last night, after his death was on the news.'

'And?'

'Do you remember when Lloyd was trying to get the local councillors to lift the speed limit in the high street? Before he knocked Joan down.'

'Yes. Didn't he dig up a load of research from groups who oppose speed cameras and zebra crossings?'

'That's right. I never even knew opposing speed cameras was a thing. But it was his first defence. He claimed that low speed limits cause as many accidents as high ones because they foster dangerous driving. People get frustrated and either over-compensate or take risks.'

'I remember looking it up, and he was right. There's evidence supporting both sides of the argument.'

'He said drivers can just about cope with going 40 MPH in built-up areas, and around hazards, but if they're made to drive at 20 MPH, it's counter-productive.'

'Thing is, no-one expected the whole village to be 20 MPH; just where the school is and along the part of the high street where the road and pavement are narrow. The fact he ran Joan over on the zebra crossing by the school showed his arguments were rubbish. He wasn't frustrated by the crossing. He was being a selfish, entitled so-and-so, who thought he could argue for one thing and do as he pleased.'

'Exactly. Then, he put forward the argument that Lower Wootton isn't a tiny seaside village any longer, with cutesy cobbled streets and horse-drawn carriages. Where people retire to.'

'That's true though.'

'He said people aren't walking to work in the village. They're commuting to London.'

Ellie scrunched up her nose. 'I don't agree with that argument, do you? I mean, yes, society has changed. Wootton has changed a bit but not that much. A lot of us do still work locally, and we've got a thriving high street which people access on foot and by car.'

'And people don't need to drive faster past hazards just because they've got to travel to London,' said Sally indignantly. 'That's their choice. It's a bit entitled to expect other people to go quicker because you feel you've got important places to get to.'

'Anyway – didn't Lloyd work locally himself? So, he can't even have believed what he was saying. He was just regurgitating some stuff he'd read on the internet and using it opportunistically because he wanted to speed through the village.'

'Going back to his sister, Lydia was part of the committee that objected to his proposals on safety grounds. She said that people coming into the doctor's surgery would get knocked over. The elderly, people with kids, folk on crutches...'

'Fran at the pet shop was on that committee too,' Ellie continued. 'She was worried about the safety of the families going into the shop to see the animals. Coming out distracted about whatever pet they wanted to buy and getting knocked over by a lunatic racing down the road.'

'Yes, and lots of local parents objected too. The council was running a campaign. What was it called now? "Help our children walk and cycle to school", wasn't it? They were offering all sorts of incentives to encourage the kids. Cycling proficiency badges through the Scouts and Girl Guides. Free bike repair kits.'

'Sylvia told me that Age Concern have a new scheme running, encouraging family members to get their oldies walking with them. It's something like: "the family dog isn't the only one who benefits from walking to school. Take Grandma and Grandad too".'

'What? On their leads?'

They both giggled.

'It's hard to understand how anyone can object to sensible speed limits without coming across as a selfish pig.'

'That's how most people saw Lloyd.' Sally moved a branch out of their way. 'When he knocked Joan down on the crossing, and it came out he was over the limit, Lydia went ballistic. Called him irresponsible, reckless and a murderer on local television.'

'I remember that. It was quite something given she's his sister. Set off a family feud. Arthur wasn't happy with her saying all that. Said she was being disloyal and had brought shame on the family.'

Sally tutted. 'Talk about blinkers. The person bringing shame on the family was the one who killed a pensioner.'

'What about Amy?'

'I liked her. We didn't know her well though, did we, even though she was in our year?'

A black and white collie came into view, a tall-framed man behind.

'Here's Ian now.' Ellie called Rebus and Luna and got her treats out. The two dogs charged towards her and slid to a halt, sitting on their bottoms, beautifully upright and attentive, waiting for the reward which Ellie duly gave them. 'Hello, Ian. Would your dog like a treat?'

'That's very kind. Thank you.' He was dressed casually, jeans, a lumberjack shirt over a white t-shirt, and a padded gilet on top.

Sally dispensed the treat and fussed the dogs while Ellie focused on Ian.

'How are you doing? You've heard about Lloyd, no doubt?'

He nodded. 'I have.'

Ellie caught the strain in his voice.

'Can't say I'm bothered about that man after what he did to Mum. Should never have been released, in my opinion. It was an absolute insult, his sentence. People shouldn't be allowed to plead guilty when there's incontrovertible evidence against them. He only did it to reduce his tariff.'

'I was so sorry about your mum. We all still are in the village. She was much loved.'

'Thank you. We miss her every day. She was a very special lady. The kids using the zebra crossing adored her.'

Ellie was trying to decide whether to be honest about needing to help Dave or whether to pretend to have a casual conversation. Thanks to Katie Douglas, and the local newspaper, everyone was going to know Dave had been arrested. But Ian might not have seen the article yet. And if he had any useful information, he'd be likely to clam up if he knew they were investigating, and she would blow her chance.

'I expect it was extremely hard for all of you when Lloyd was released?'

'It was. Scumbag like him, should've rotted in there. I knew they'd release him early. I wrote to the prison governor, putting my concerns, but he said the early release is automatic. There's no review. No risk assessment.'

'Crazy.'

'And Lloyd must've lied through his teeth, as the governor said he was full of remorse and posed no threat of repeat offending.'

'Dreadful. Did you see him after his release?'

He nodded. 'It's why I didn't want him to come back to Wootton. You know what it's like round here. We all use the same shops and pub. We're bumping into people all the time and it's really awkward when they're the last person you want to see.'

Ellie understood completely. After Dave's affair, she was regularly encountering him and getting stirred up each time. She'd seriously contemplated moving away.

'I thought I saw Lloyd at the petrol station last week. That bird's nest hair of his and the annoying laugh. My head filled with rage.' He clamped his hands over his face. 'He wasn't in a vehicle, but the thought of that man defying his ban, getting back behind the wheel and running someone else over...' He strode restlessly back and forth, as though he couldn't bear what his mind was contemplating.

'What did you do?' asked Sally.

'I didn't trust myself. I got back in my car and locked the doors. Put my head on the steering wheel and waited for him to go. The garage owner came out. Thought I'd fainted or had a heart attack or something.'

Ellie was weighing up what Ian was telling them. She was inclined to believe him. It was an awful situation to be in. To lose your mother so cruelly and then have to face her killer around the village after such a short sentence. But she had to be objective. To keep an open mind. Could desperation have pushed Ian to get rid of Lloyd? To exact revenge?

What had he said? 'The thought of that man defying his ban…' There was no getting away from the fact that Lloyd had been stopped from doing anything again.

'Have the police spoken to you?' Ellie knew they would have but hoped it would prompt Ian to share what they'd discussed.

'Of course. I'm sure I was their number one suspect.' A look flickered across his face. 'Although I think they've got someone else in the frame now.'

Dave.

'Did they ask you for an alibi for yesterday morning?'

He nodded. 'Fortunately, I'm in the clear. My missus. We got up at the usual time, 6.30am, and walked the dog together. It was her day off. We saw your Finn, as it goes, running with Charlie Matthews.'

That would be easy to check. And would've been around this time.

'Who else in your family was angry with Lloyd?'

'Do you mean, who else might have wanted to bump him off?'

Ellie smiled.

'We are all still very raw. But I'm the one who was most vocal, as you probably remember. I admitted I wanted him dead for what he did. But thinking about it and wanting it are very different to actually killing him.' He paused. 'No way I was going to ruin my life for that piece of scum.'

She knew that was the rational view. It's what any killer would say who wanted to deny their actions. They'd invoke reason and logic. But what if Ian had lost control? Seen red and in a moment of madness had lashed out at Lloyd? Perhaps seeing him again had tipped him over the edge? She wasn't sure what to make of it.

'Who do you think might have killed him?' Ellie asked gently.

He snorted. 'Take your pick. Even before he murdered my mum, he'd had run-ins with half the village. My missus will tell you. That stupid scheme of his to get speed limits lifted in the village and to get the zebra crossing moved so he could tear up and down the high street in that battered old van of his.'

'Sally and I were just talking about this. The pet shop opposed his proposal, didn't they? And the doctor's surgery?'

'Yes. All the shop owners at that end of the village. He tried to intimidate every one of them.' His face creased into a smile. 'Came a cropper when he tried it with Nick Matthews though, didn't he?'

'I'd forgotten about that.'

The Matthews' shop was in that area. Ellie would see what Nick knew. He would've had a view about the speed limit along the high street. There'd been regular discussions over the years about whether to pedestrianise that stretch of the village. It was one of those topics that surfaced at intervals, quickly got mired in complexity and indecision, and came back up when someone else thought it would be a good idea.

'Anyone else dislike him apart from the group opposing that scheme?' asked Ellie.

'You know his sister called him out, don't you? Lydia. Disowned him. Very kind to my family, she was.'

'Yes. It was brave of her. Have you kept in touch with her?'

'Not really. When Lloyd went to prison, we all tried to get on with life. We couldn't get the judge to increase the sentence...' His words petered out.

'Presumably she knew he was being released?'

'Oh yes. She told me before the police did. Came straight round, told my missus.'

Ian collected up the dog's lead and Ellie sensed he was wanting to go.

'Where does Lydia live? I know she works at the doctor's surgery.'

'She sold her house and has been renting the flat above the surgery while she decided where she wanted to live.'

'Ah, OK. Thanks.' She smiled at Ian. 'Take care, then, won't you?'

He was about to continue his walk when he stopped. 'Since you were asking about people with grudges against Lloyd... you do know he and Dave had an almighty set-to the other day, don't you?'

'No, I didn't. When was this?'

'Last week.'

Chapter 11

The windmill smelled of toast and coffee when Ellie arrived home from the woods with Rebus. As soon as she let the dog off his lead, he went bounding over to Dave, who was at the table, spreading peanut butter onto toast. A kitten was on his lap, chewing one of his shirt buttons.

'Zoe slept at Finn's,' he said helpfully. 'She didn't leave the club 'til around two. Didn't want to wake up everyone here, and Finn doesn't mind. She's on her way over.'

'Thanks,' said Ellie, with a twinge of *déjà vu*. It was almost like old times, before Dave's affair. Coming home, him there, catching up on family things.

Except Dave was under investigation for murder. It was all over the local newspaper, and she'd just learnt he'd lied to her.

Rebus jumped up to greet Dave and got a whack on the nose from the resident kitten.

'Did Sophie go with Zoe to Finn's?' Ellie felt a twinge of protectiveness. 'She didn't come home to the pet shop last night.'

She told him about the neighbours' comments.

'Didn't say.'

'I'll ask Zo.' She was resisting to urge to blurt out what she'd learnt. To accuse him. 'Does she know you're out of custody?' she said instead.

'Yep,' Dave replied. 'I texted her.'

'There's coffee in the pot.' Sylvia was at the mirror by the door, putting in earrings. 'I'm leaving in twenty minutes.' She began applying lipstick.

But Ian's comment was ringing in Ellie's ears, and she wanted answers. What had Dave and Lloyd rowed about recently? And why had Dave told her he hadn't seen – or been in contact with – Lloyd since his release from prison?

'I was going to ask Sally for breakfast, but wanted a chat with you and Dave before you go to church,' she said in Sylvia's direction.

'You'll have to be quick then,' she replied through pouting lips.

'I am here, you know,' said Dave grumpily.

Ellie grabbed a mug from the cupboard and poured herself a coffee. 'Sally and I bumped into Ian in the woods,' she told them.

'Oh, right.' He paused. 'What did he have to say?'

'That's what I want to ask you about. He said you and Lloyd had a row recently.' She sat down next to him and stared at him.

'Ah.'

'Which I found odd because you told me you haven't seen him since he came out of prison or had contact with him.'

A mixture of fear and annoyance twisted in her belly. They were all worried sick about Dave. Were wracking their brains for why he could have been arrested and how they could help him. Feeling horribly guilty for wondering – out of sheer fear for the future – if there was something else, something Dave wasn't telling them.

And here they were.

'So, if you want us to help you, could you tell us the *truth*, please?' Ellie's heart was thumping in her chest. Dave didn't lie often – as far as she knew – but she had the same reaction whenever he did.

He sighed.

She stirred her coffee, feeling slightly nauseous.

'At the time it happened, I didn't mention it because it was over and done with,' he said, 'and you weren't there to tell.'

'Did you tell your police colleagues you'd seen him? Given that Lloyd had threatened you with revenge before he went to prison.'

'Yes. I mentioned it to the chief inspector in an email so it was on record, but what Lloyd did wasn't illegal so there was no action that could be taken.' He took a sip of coffee. 'Then, when you asked me about it yesterday, I didn't say anything because I didn't want to worry you.'

Sylvia sat down on the other side of Dave. She had her compact out and was applying mascara. 'I think you're going to have to do better than that.'

'You beat me to it,' said Ellie. 'You didn't want to worry me? That's so patronising.'

'I knew there would be speculation, because of my role in his conviction, and I knew it would worry you. I didn't want to add to that.' He placed his toast back on the plate and sat back in his seat, Ellie one side of him, his mother the other.

Ellie wasn't sure how she felt about this statement. 'There are a lot of assumptions in what you've just said.' The implications were falling into place, pushing her buttons because the situation reminded her of when Dave hadn't been honest about his brief affair with Finn's mother. It was to do with the steady trickle of information through third parties.

A frown flickered across Dave's face.

'Caring about my feelings and empathising are one thing,' Ellie continued. 'What you did was decide what I should and shouldn't know. I'm not sure I like that.'

'If that's how it came across, I'm sorry. I was annoyed I'd seen him. I wanted him to – it sounds stupid now but – get married and go off on his honeymoon without either of us seeing each other.'

Ellie frowned. This wasn't typical Dave behaviour at all. 'I'm glad you realise how ridiculous that seems. How did you think the two of you were going to avoid each other after that?'

He shrugged.

That wasn't typical Dave behaviour either. He was usually Mr Think Ahead; Mr Contingency. 'We all live in the same village.'

Silence from Dave.

'What happened then? Where did you meet?' Ellie was envisaging the pub or the newsagent. A chance meeting somewhere busy where they both happened to converge.

'Lloyd turned up at my flat one evening last week, drunk.'

'You're kidding?'

'Nope. Chuntering away about a load of unintelligible rubbish. Saying he knew what I'd done, and he was going to make sure I paid for it.'

'Threatening you, then.'

Dave nodded.

'What did he think you'd done? Was it relating to his conviction or something new?'

'He didn't say. It was drunken ranting. Could barely make out what he was muttering.'

'Did he have a weapon or anything?'

'No. Just a half bottle of spirits which he was waving around and swigging from at intervals.'

'What did you do?'

'Told him to sling his hook.' His expression shifted from annoyance to relief. 'At first, I was irritated by the intrusion but fortunately realised he was only saying it to wind me up. Maybe even provoke me. Who knows?'

'And?'

'Eventually, he left. Shuffled off still mumbling and cursing.'

'Surely coming round, uninvited, to someone's house, drunk, and threatening them is an offence?'

'It's a grey area. Saying you're going to make someone "pay" isn't specific. A threat to kill is against the law.'

Ellie was finding it hard to process what Dave was telling them. He could be a bit hot-headed sometimes, but not where work was concerned. Denying he'd seen Lloyd when she asked him seemed out of character. Or was she simply biased because she loved him – or had done, at one time?

'This isn't making sense,' she said.

'Nor to me,' said Sylvia. She blotted her lipstick on a tissue.

'Did anyone see Lloyd at Goose Meadow?' asked Ellie.

'Yes. He rang a couple of the building's doorbells, I gather, before he got mine. And some of the neighbours heard him shouting. The lady in the flat opposite stuck her head out of her front door, wondering what the commotion was. Her husband is friends with Joan's son. I've seen him round there a lot. That's probably how he knows what happened.'

There were witnesses then. That was good.

Ellie was annoyed about Dave's lie and couldn't decide whether Lloyd having threatened him made Dave's situation with the police worse or didn't make any real difference. Inside her head, a voice kept whispering: what if more had taken place than Dave was telling them? What if Dave *had* threatened Lloyd? It would be useful to speak to one of the witnesses at the building. See whether their version of events tallied with Dave's.

'We can talk further about this later. I'm aware of the time and your mum needing to go.' What she wanted was a chat alone with Sylvia, to get her sense of things.

'Speaking of which,' said Sylvia, 'and I'm not stirring here but you haven't mentioned it.' She nudged Dave with her elbow. 'Don't you need to tell Ellie about the... er... *new* evidence?'

Dave groaned and filled Ellie in.

Ellie stared at him as he spoke, her nostrils flaring, heart thumping in her chest.

'I know what you're going to say,' he said.

She was on her feet. 'Go on, then, mind-reader.' Her voice dripped with sarcasm.

'You're going to ask if there's something *else* I haven't told you.'

'What part of "you've got to be honest with us" do you not understand? Well, is there anything else?'

'No. And I don't know *anything* about the trainers or the wire. I was *not* at the pond. I have *no* idea how blood got on my trainers and the wire isn't mine. I was going to tell you about all of it but didn't want to do it when you were already annoyed with me.'

'*Annoyed?* For goodness' sake, Dave. Grow up. We're not at school. You haven't copied my homework without my permission or broken my favourite pencil. Someone's been killed.'

'My thoughts exactly,' Sylvia mumbled into her mirror.

'That's helpful,' Dave snapped at his mum.

Ellie continued. 'You've been arrested on suspicion of murder and now I'm beginning to understand why you've been released under investigation rather than with no further action.' Her stomach lurched and a wave of nausea swept over her. 'With that amount of evidence, surely the CPS could recommend charging you?'

'Wow,' he said. 'Thanks. Are you sure you don't think I killed him?'

'I don't know what to think,' she snapped. 'Right now, I'm wondering what the next bit of information is going to be. I'm half-expecting you to say that someone saw you in the hare meadow in the early hours. And you didn't mention it because you didn't want to worry me.'

'Oh, that's charming, that is. Now you're being ridiculous.'

'OK, you two,' Sylvia interjected. 'That's enough. Let's return to the subject of the trainers and the picture wire when I get back.' She put her hand on Dave's shoulders. 'It was good that you documented that Lloyd had been round to your house. Did the chief inspector reply to your email?'

Dave nodded. 'He said to keep my head down as Lloyd was going away and we'd discuss it further then.'

Sylvia and Ellie caught each other's eye.

'Surely the time to discuss it was straight after he'd been round?' Sylvia had her headmistress-y tone on. 'Get a police officer to speak to him, tell him to stay away from you or there would need to be a court order?'

Dave cast his gaze down to his plate and his uneaten toast. 'With hindsight, perhaps, but–'

'Look, if you want us to help you, you've *got* to be straight with us. I don't know how much plainer I can be.' Ellie tried to keep her voice soft but was finding it hard. As the conversation had been progressing, it'd been freaking her out. 'I don't want to keep discovering things you haven't told us. Quite apart from the effect it's having on my trust in you...'

Dave winced.

'... it's making me worry that the police will be back at the door any minute saying they're going to charge you with murder.' Her stomach somersaulted as she said the word.

'I feel the same,' said Sylvia. 'It's not on.'

'And Zoe is not coping well. She was very upset earlier. Terrified you're going to prison.'

'I understand that,' muttered Dave. 'I'm sorry.'

Ellie had her hands on her hips. 'So? Is there anything else you haven't told us?'

He shook his head. 'I'm sorry, Ells. I know it might've been clumsy, but I genuinely didn't tell you Lloyd had come round because I didn't want to worry you.'

Ellie didn't respond. 'Moving on then. I've spoken to Ian already,' she continued, aware she was still annoyed with Dave but also wanted to make the most of the time. 'We're planning to talk to Arthur, Amy and Lydia today.'

'Uh-huh.'

'You obviously can't come with us, but is there anything we should add into our questioning that you know about, and we might not?'

Ellie was aware this was a novel situation. Ever since they'd started Blix Investigators, the dynamic with Dave had been tense. To start with he'd been really annoyed by their sleuthing – and with some justification. Over the months, and four cases, he'd begun to accept that Ellie was psychologically driven to help people she cared about. But – he'd always stuck to procedure and been careful not to pass on information which was sensitive to police investigations.

'I'm also going to ask Leonard what he knows about Amy and Lloyd,' added Sylvia. Her neck had flecks of red, and Ellie wondered how she felt about the conversation they'd been having.

The front door opened, and Zoe burst in. ‘Dad.’ She shot over and threw her arms round him. ‘I’m so pleased you’re out. Are you going to stay here for a bit?’

‘I... I was going to ask if I could hang here today?’ He glanced at Ellie nervously. ‘I’ve been instructed not to go back to the flat just yet, and certainly don’t want to sit there on my own, fretting over whether I’m going to lose my job.’

‘You can stay here with us.’ Zoe’s face was animated. She still had her arms round Dave’s neck and was gazing at him adoringly. ‘Mum’s sleeping at the pet shop with the kittens so you can sleep in her bed.’

‘Er... Excuse me,’ said Ellie. ‘Do I get a say in this?’ She’d given her bedroom a complete makeover when Dave had his affair. Reclaimed it for herself.

‘I’m not sure about that, Zo.’ He gave Ellie an apologetic look. ‘But it’d be good to hang here until bed.’

‘That’s fine, isn’t it, Mum?’ She slid her arm off Dave’s neck. ‘You can sleep in my bed, Dad. I can bunk in with Mum or Gran.’

‘We’ll discuss that later.’ Ellie lifted Zoe’s plait affectionately. ‘Let’s finish what we were discussing about the investigation.’

'What have I missed?' asked Zoe.

'We'll fill you in shortly,' said Dave. 'First though – where's Sophie?'

'She came home with me. I've left her at Finn's.'

'What was she doing 'til 4am the night before your mum started pet-sitting? Did she say?' He explained that, with Fran away, they'd been worried by the neighbours' comments.

'She went to a house party.' Zoe rolled her eyes. 'She's a singer and does some DJ-ing. So, she goes where the gigs are. Hangs out with musicians. Those neighbours disapprove of her lifestyle. That's all.'

'That's up to them,' said Dave, 'but there's a killer on the loose, and I'm concerned about everyone's safety. So, I don't want you out late on your own. Yes?'

'Yeah, Dad.'

'And see if you can have a word with Sophie, too,' he said. 'OK. Going back to Leonard – I was about to speak to him when I got kicked off the case.' His voice was quiet, as though he was embarrassed. 'As the local vicar, and the person who was marrying Lloyd and Amy, he would have got to know them quite well. They would have had meetings to discuss their vows, their feelings, the ceremony. They would've had rehearsals.'

'Exactly,' said Sylvia.

'I can't think of anything specific to ask him. I'm sure you'll pick up on anything relevant, Mum. But the more information you can get out of him, the better.'

'Great. Thanks.'

'What about Lloyd's dad?'

'Arthur is a weird one.' Dave's tone was more confident now. 'I was rather surprised by his staunch support of his son.' He seemed to be picking his words carefully. 'I would have expected him to come down hard on Lloyd. The drink driving. The death that resulted. Particularly since he and Joan were friends.'

'It is odd,' Sylvia chipped in, 'but not unheard of. Filial bonds can be very strong. Especially since Arthur's a widower.'

Dave nodded. 'And before that, Lloyd's campaign to get the speed limit lifted in the village. Arthur used to take the kids to school before he went to work. He'd shuffle over that pedestrian crossing every day and chat to Joan. I remember it clearly. We'd all be walking home, and he'd stop for a laugh and a joke with the lollipop lady.'

He was shaking his head. 'I could never understand why he wasn't disgusted by Lloyd's behaviour.' He paused. 'Maybe you can ask him how he *really* felt about his son's actions.'

'Hold on,' said Ellie. 'Are we thinking about Arthur as a suspect or a witness?'

'At the moment – a witness, surely?' replied Sylvia. 'But we don't know, do we? We are simply following leads at this stage. After all, why would he want to kill his own son?'

'What about Amy and Lydia?' asked Ellie. 'We'll need to be careful with Amy. And maybe wait a while before we speak to her. She must be devastated.'

'Lydia is potentially a good source of information because she refused to buy into pressure for family loyalty,' said Dave. 'She'll also have an idea of who else was against her brother at the various stages of things. The campaign, the death, his release.'

'That's a good point,' said Ellie.

'Possibly even things she didn't tell the police. But Lydia won't know the sorts of things that Amy will know because she and Lloyd were estranged, and she wasn't privy to family discussions about him.' He tapped his fingers on the table.

'Yes, they'll both have very different perspectives,' said Ellie.

Dave continued. 'Something we haven't discussed is the murder method. When you're considering suspects, and interviewing them, have a think about who might be capable of garrotting someone with picture wire.'

'It's a vicious way of ending a person's life, isn't it?' replied Ellie.

'Kinda rules out a crime of passion too,' Zoe added, returning from the fridge with a tub of yoghurt. 'I mean, who walks around with picture wire in their pocket?' She gasped. 'Dad, did the cops show you the wire they found?'

'Yes, why?'

'What did it look like?'

'Yellowy-golden colour. Not on a spool but wound into a circle and in a small resealable plastic bag with red on it.'

'It might be a long shot but what if the killer got it from the hardware shop in the village? One of us should pop in.'

'That's a good idea,' said Dave. 'The killer might not have wanted to order it online as there'd be a record of their address.'

'Right.' Sylvia snapped her bag shut. 'On that note, I need to love you and leave you. If there are any developments, text me.' She threw a glance at Ellie and Dave. 'Can I trust you two not to have a row while I'm out?'

Chapter 12

After the church service, Sylvia hung around to speak to the vicar about Amy and Lloyd. She was still chewing over the conversation she and Ellie had just had with Dave. In particular, Lloyd turning up at Dave's flat.

Like Ellie, she was finding it difficult to be objective. To separate her maternal loyalty from her assessment of events. Dave's behaviour worried her, and she had a sinking feeling, not just that things weren't at all right. That there was worse to come.

In addition, guilt was like a stone in her shoe, bothering her whenever she questioned the account her son had given. How could she have doubts about Dave?

That was as bad as the worry itself.

Of course, his liberty was most important, but she could also see the career he'd worked so hard at disintegrating in front of him if he wasn't careful.

And Ellie came to mind again too.

She'd watched the two of them navigate their way round Dave's affair. Seen Ellie's trust begin to redevelop. Felt how much they both loved each other. Now, just as he'd turned down the offer of promotion in Birmingham, and it looked like a reconciliation might be possible, all this had happened.

Sylvia and Leonard were in the kitchen at the Rectory, washing up after the increasingly popular post-service tea and coffee. Sylvia's hands were sloshing about in the soapy water.

Leonard had a yellow apron over his black top and trousers. On it was a hazard sign and the words: *WARNING. Man cooking.*

He had a tea towel in his hand and was drying each item with meticulous care.

'Your chocolate fudge tray bake went down well, didn't it?' he said. 'Was that caramelised brown sugar you put on top of the sponge?'

'Thank you. Yes. With a *soupçon* of black treacle. Adds to the sweetness and depth of taste. Something I got from one of Mum's recipes.'

Sylvia enjoyed her baking conversations with Leonard and this morning they were a welcome distraction from her worries about Dave, even though she wanted to ask him about Lloyd and Amy. She'd never met a man who enjoyed his cooking as much as he did. Her late husband, Ron, had always appreciated his wife's creativity in the kitchen – and enjoyed eating the output – but had never shown any desire to get the scales out himself and experiment. Perhaps because he'd always worked such long hours, and away from the home. A lot of Leonard's days were spent at the Rectory, talking to his parishioners and hosting them. It was lucky he liked baking.

'I was pleased to see some of Joan's family at the service this morning. I've been praying for them *and* for Lloyd's family too.'

'It's a terrible thing to happen.' She gathered her thoughts as she rinsed a handful of spoons and laid them on the draining board. 'I expect Lloyd and Amy were excited about their wedding, were they?'

What she wanted to know was how they got on, but it seemed a bit of an insensitive thing to ask, and she wasn't sure how Leonard would respond.

He smiled. 'Very much so. It had been keeping them both going since he was sent to prison.'

Sylvia picked up on the word 'both.' 'That's nice. They must've been very much in love then.'

'Oh, yes. She said he had redeeming qualities.'

Sylvia bit her lip. She was about to express her surprise, and caught herself. 'That's an interesting term for her to use. Isn't it?' She tried to gauge Leonard's face for his reaction. 'It implies Lloyd had qualities that weren't appealing.'

Leonard picked up a glass and dried it with a tea-towel. 'She was pretty down to earth about him. She knew a lot of people didn't like him. But said they didn't know him like she did.'

'That's fair enough, I guess. I suppose I'm just a bit curious. I can't imagine marrying someone who'd behaved so cruelly and selfishly. And who'd killed another person. Did she talk to you about that?'

He nodded. 'Yes. A great deal. Amy's aunt Belinda was vehemently against her marrying Lloyd. She thought he was a... well, I'm not going to repeat her words as they aren't godly. Let's just say she had an extremely low opinion of Lloyd and was convinced he would ruin Amy's life.'

'I see. That must've been difficult for Amy.' She was following a train of thought in her mind. 'So, she and Lloyd had a lot in common really. A shared history. And they both had family members who were dead against decisions they'd made.'

Leonard cringed as she said the word 'dead'.

'What I meant was, Lydia disapproved of Lloyd's behaviour and Belinda was against Amy's decision. Did you get a sense of them feeling like it was "us against the world"?'

'Oh, definitely. I talked to them together and separately. I always do that with couples who are tying the knot. Sometimes there are things one doesn't want to say in front of the other, and I need to know if there are any impediments, lawful or otherwise. But on this topic, they agreed. It was definitely them against the world.'

Sylvia had had social work clients who'd been in similar situations, and it was often clear that when family members had been against their partners, it had the effect of pushing them together more. And the more people tried to split them up, the more determined they were to stay a couple.

'But that wasn't all they had between them, was it? The desire not to be dictated to?'

Leonard stopped wiping for a moment and held the plate still in his hand. 'I must admit, I did wonder about that to start with, but when I got talking to them both, I realised they genuinely had a strong bond. They'd known each other for over thirty years. Since primary school.'

Sylvia briefly thought of Ellie and Dave. They'd known each other for years too. And although they weren't a couple at the moment, it was obvious they loved each other deeply. She did hope this awful business wasn't going to scupper their chances of a reconciliation. 'When you talked to Lloyd, did you get the impression he was sorry for what he did?'

Leonard drew in a deep breath. 'It was very hard to know for sure.' He stood still for a few moments, holding the plate he was drying, as though he was sifting through his thoughts and feelings. 'As a Christian, I believe in redemption and forgiveness. And that people can change. He said he had. He expressed deep regret.' His voice trailed off.

'But?'

'I think the "but" is simply what I've said. In this sort of situation, when someone is released from prison, they can tell you all sorts of things and it's extremely hard to know if they genuinely understand what they're saying and mean them.'

Sylvia nodded. She knew this to be true from her social work clients. Often, they'd sworn on their mother's or their granny's or their favourite pet's lives they'd changed; they were sorry, they would never repeat their actions. Some kept to their word, others didn't.

'The thing is,' she said, 'they usually have a lot riding on things going well. They want a fresh start. They don't want to go back to prison. They want people to believe them and give them the benefit of the doubt.'

'Lloyd knew that coming back to Lower Wootton wouldn't be easy,' said Leonard pensively. 'But he had family here – especially his father – and his fiancée, and he was determined it was what he wanted.'

'He was perfectly entitled to come back to the village. It's a dreadful shame that he did, though. Someone was clearly not happy about it.'

'I must admit, that went through my mind when I heard the news. If only he and Amy had got married and gone to live somewhere else. It's always difficult when someone who's committed a crime like his returns to live amongst the people he's hurt.'

'Did he say if anyone was threatening him? Or giving him a hard time?'

'Yes. He did.' He paused again. 'I'm really sorry, Sylvia. You're not going to like this.'

Sylvia's heart lurched.

'I've been trying to find the right time to tell you ever since I heard. Then Dave was arrested. I know how worried you are and didn't want to make things worse for you.'

'Oh, my goodness. Not you too with that "I was protecting you" line. Whatever is it?'

'I say.' He stood still, a wounded expression in his eyes. 'That's a bit much. What do you mean?'

She explained about Dave using a similar expression.

'OK. Let's talk about this.' He dried his hands, took off the apron and gestured to the table.

Sylvia couldn't ignore him and carry on washing up, so she followed suit and sat down with him.

'What I've learnt from the scriptures is that there's a difference between keeping a secret from someone to control them,' he said, in his kind voice, 'and reflecting on whether it is helpful, kind and true to share information. And thinking about the timing of the news.'

Sylvia wasn't religious but she couldn't help agreeing with him.

'I had every intention of telling you what I learnt, but I also wanted to pick a good time.' He smiled. 'Unfortunately, sometimes there isn't a good time and you get pipped to the post.'

She explained how hard it was, knowing Dave had kept secrets from Ellie.

'As long as you know I'm not your son. Deal?'

'Deal. I'm sorry I snapped. What were you going to tell me?'

'That Lloyd said Dave had been threatening him.' Through the lenses of his glasses, Leonard's eyes looked huge. He dropped his voice to a whisper. 'Not just that, though. He was scared Dave was going to kill him. Said he was *scared for his life.*'

Chapter 13

Ellie rolled up her yoga mat and pulled the band round it. She let out a deep sigh. Her body was looser, and she felt taller.

After the revelations about Dave, she'd needed some exercise, a physical and mental release. She'd managed the Sun Salutations today without collapsing, and hadn't done a 'botty burp' – as Sylvia called them – in Downward Dog.

'Amy?' Ellie couldn't contain her surprise. She shuffled over to the woman. 'How... How are you?'

It was still early. Had Amy seen Katie's piece in the local paper?

In the vast space of the community centre hall, their words sounded loud. The floor to ceiling windows enhanced the 'empty warehouse' effects.

Hand pan music wafted round the room. It was the instructor's new thing.

'Oh, hi.' Amy's voice was floaty. 'Pretty awful.'

She pulled a faint smile on her make-up-less face. Did that mean she hadn't seen the article?

'Mum dragged me down here this morning. Said it might get my *chi* moving, whatever that is. I didn't move from the sofa yesterday. Or eat.'

She couldn't have seen it yet, surely? She wouldn't be this friendly.

In addition to Ellie's concerns about Dave, it was impossible not to feel the pain in Amy's reply and Ellie realised she needed to tread sensitively. It wasn't clear whether Amy knew Dave had been arrested and she was interested to know what she knew about Dave and Lloyd's recent interactions.

'I'm really sorry about Lloyd. It must be a terrible shock. I'll walk back with you, if you like.'

'Sure. Why not? The vet's practice has insisted I have some time off so I'm grateful for any distraction.' She sniffed. 'I'll just text Mum, let her know I'm on my way home.' She got her phone out of her pocket and tapped away at the keyboard. 'Lloyd and I were meant to be going on our honeymoon today.' Her eyes brimmed with tears. 'The Lake District. We had a cabin booked. Lloyd was looking forward to doing some fishing, and I was going to read.'

Ellie nodded. 'If I can help...' She put her arm round Amy. 'C'mon. Let's walk, shall we?'

They were soon outside, heading towards the high street. To Ellie, it was a beautiful morning, sun rising in a blue sky that was streaked with grey, but she was aware that to Amy it must feel like another cruel day.

Ellie marshalled her thoughts.

'Do you have any idea who might have done this?' She was dreading Amy saying 'Dave'.

Amy shook her head. 'The cops asked me that exact question and the truth is, I have no idea. So many people were against him, Ells. And I understand why, but...' She broke off. 'He went out for a few drinks in Deal on Friday night with his dad and a couple of mates. We were due to meet at the church the next morning. That's the last I saw of him.' She let out a sob. 'He texted me to say he was having a great evening and he loved me. I had a glass of fizz with my sister and Mum. Hung up my dress and laid out my shoes. And went to sleep. The next thing I knew, the police were at the door.'

'Was anyone against you marrying Lloyd?' They knew about her aunt, Belinda, and Lloyd's sister, Lydia, but she wanted to see what Amy would say.

'Sadly, yes.' She cited Belinda and Lydia.

'Tell me about your aunt. Do you know why?' Ellie was wondering whether it was to do with Joan's death or from before that.

'She said he was bad news and that I would regret being with him.'

That was a bit vague. Perhaps they could track Belinda down, find out what her objections were.

'Presumably Belinda knew you two were getting married?'

Amy nodded. 'She refused to come to the wedding.'

'What about Lydia?'

'Similar actually. She thought he'd cause me grief.'

'It must've been difficult with so many people against him?'

She gave a sad nod.

Ellie wanted to ask whether Amy knew about Dave threatening Lloyd, but it didn't seem fair or appropriate.

And it would be obvious that Ellie was fishing for information. Could she assume that, as Amy hadn't mentioned threats from Dave, she didn't know about them? Or didn't consider them to have been serious? It was hard to tell.

'Are your mum and sister going to stay with you for a bit? You won't be on your own, will you?'

They were in the high street now. Most of the shops were closed on Sundays. Ellie caught a waft of coffee and sugar as they approached the bakery café. They'd opened up the ice cream hatch and were selling drinks and hot cross buns. She waved at the owner, who was behind the hatch.

'Can I get you a cuppa and a croissant, or something? At least you'll have had breakfast then.' Ellie got a twenty pound note out of her bum-bag and walked towards the serving hatch.

'Oh, that's very kind. I...'

'What would you like?'

'Just a latte, please. No food. I can't eat at the moment.'

Ellie ordered their drinks, and paid, and they carried on walking.

'What did you ask me?' said Amy.

'If anyone's staying with you.'

'Yes. Mum is. My sister has her kids and husband, so she'll pop in and out, when she can. Lloyd's father, Arthur, is going to do the formal identification. I haven't decided if I want to see Lloyd before he's cremated.'

'That's good. It gives you a bit of time to decide.'

Amy faced Ellie, fixing her eyes on hers. 'You know, Lloyd said something weird in the days before he died.'

Ellie's ears pricked up.

'He said he was sure someone was watching him.' She paused. 'Said it three or four times. Watching him or following him. He was convinced it was to do with Joan's death.'

Ellie paused.

'I got the impression it was a woman,' Amy continued. 'I can't help thinking about the two who've been so against him.'

Ellie listened carefully.

'Do you think it could've been my aunt? Or Lloyd's sister, Lydia?'

Chapter 14

As Sylvia drew closer to Arthur Durden's house, her trepidation increased. She had a feeling the interview was either going to be fine – or be a nightmare, depending on whether he knew Dave had been arrested.

Hopefully, it would help that they knew each other from bell-ringing and were both parents of children who'd been to the same school.

Arthur was in his front garden with a spade, digging up a fuchsia that had gone woody and lost all its leaves. He spotted her walking up the path.

'You've got a cheek, coming round here.' He pulled his cloth cap down and sliced the spade into the ground, wiggling it round the shrub's roots.

He knew.

'He's been released,' Sylvia told him.

'That doesn't mean anything, and you know it.' He carried on digging. 'He's a copper. They're probably trying to fit someone else up for it. Protecting their own.'

'He didn't do it, Arthur.'

'You would say that, wouldn't you? He's your son.'

Sylvia was tempted to say, 'Like you defended yours when he ran Joan down?' but stopped herself. 'I said it because I believe it,' she said instead. 'I know he's my son but he's a good man.'

He was leaning on the spade now, studying the sinewy bark of the deceased bush, as though willing it to come back to life. A similar age to Sylvia, Arthur's coat-hanger frame and white hair made him seem twenty years older.

A robin swooped down from the fence and pecked at the freshly dug soil.

'Tame as anything, he is.' Arthur gestured to the bird. 'Their feeders need topping up.'

Sylvia was pleased Arthur had the garden. Hopefully, it would help with his grief.

He held up a section of the bush. 'My wife planted this not long before she died. Loved fuchsias, she did.' His gaunt face looked pained. 'Shame how things change, isn't it?'

Sylvia gave him a kind smile. She knew what it was like to lose your life partner and have to carry on living on your own.

'Look. I haven't come round here to argue,' she said softly.

'What have you come for then, eh?' He tugged at another stem in the ground.

'I wanted to see how you're doing. I'm sorry about Lloyd.'

'You don't need to pretend. Apart from Amy, and a couple of his pals, no-one liked him.'

'What have the police said?' It struck Sylvia how upsetting it must be to know how much bad feeling there was towards Lloyd.

He snorted at the mention of the police. 'They've offered me a family liaison officer, but I've said no. Don't like coppers at the best of times and I don't want anyone in the house, poking about in our things, asking questions, watching every move I make.'

'As long as you're OK alone. Could someone in the family stay with you for a few days?' It wasn't going to be Lydia. Neither of them would want that.

'I'll be alright. They're saying he was strangled, you know. With some picture wire.'

Sylvia couldn't help thinking about the wire the police had found at Dave's flat. They'd be testing it to see if it was the same kind. And what Ellie had said about it being a vicious way to end someone's life.

'I heard.' She paused. 'I gather you were out with him on Friday night for his stag drinks. Where did you all go?'

A frown flickered across his forehead. 'Cops asked that. Just local pubs, like.'

Hmm. It would be useful to know where in case they needed to check anything.

'Which ones?' She caught Arthur's pursed lips. 'Our Finn likes the Freed Man. And the ones with live music.'

Arthur relaxed a bit. 'A couple of pubs in Deal. The King's Head on the seafront and the Port Arms, then the Lighthouse and the Freed Man. Lloyd likes it...' He stopped. Swallowed. '*Liked* it there too.'

'Were there many of you?'

'Flippin' cops asked me that and all.'

'Sorry. Just interested.'

'Four of us. Two of Lloyd's mates. Chap called Steve from Dover and... can't remember the name of the other.

My memory these days. It'll come to me. Bryan? Barry, maybe?'

'When you left Lloyd, where was he going? We're trying to piece together how he got to the hare meadow.'

Arthur's eyes narrowed. 'What d'you mean "trying to piece together"? What's going on?' He walked over to her. 'Are you working with the cops or something?'

Sylvia was cursing her stupidity. She should have watched her words, been more circumspect. 'Sorry, Arthur.' She told him about Blix Investigators.

'You being paid then? Who's asked you to investigate?' He walked away from her. 'Look here. I'm not sure how I feel about you coming round here, asking me all these questions.'

She had to come clean. It felt disrespectful to keep pretending she was here for altruistic reasons.

'Dave's asked us to investigate. *Not* because he's guilty. Because he's worried about the evidence the police have found. Worried he's going to be charged for something he didn't do.' She leaned against the fence and told Arthur a little of the detail. 'We're beside ourselves. Ellie. His daughter. Me.'

'I don't know what to say. If he's done it, he'll have to go down for it. Just like Lloyd did.'

Sylvia felt herself bridling at his remark. But she bit her lip. Arthur was grieving for two family members now, his wife and his son. '*Had* Dave been threatening Lloyd, do you know?'

'Aye. That's what he told me. But you know what those two were like. Been bad blood between them since they were teenagers.'

'*Has there?*' She remembered Leonard's comment, that Lloyd had been scared for his life. 'That's news to me.' Sylvia was spooling back through her memory to when Dave was growing up.

'If I'm honest, I half expected one of them to kill the other, I did.'

Sylvia gasped. Arthur's matter-of-fact statement hit her in the solar plexus. 'Lloyd told the vicar he was scared Dave was going to kill him.'

Arthur shook his head and joined her at the fence. 'Like I said: there was bad feeling between those two.'

Sylvia felt the lurch of nausea as she tried to take in this new information. It was too much.

She changed the subject. 'You were telling me about the stag do.'

'I left him after the Freed Man. He said he was going home to get some kip, then was going to get up early and go fishing.'

'Where was he going to fish?'

'In the pond in the hare meadow, I think.'

'Amy didn't say anything about Lloyd coming home and collecting his fishing gear. Where did he keep it?'

'At her place, in the garden shed.'

'He can't have reached home then. Was he going to fish on his own?'

'As far as I know. He said it was a bit late to organise anything. Unless he made arrangements during the evening, while we were out.'

'Hmm.' Sylvia wanted to think about that. 'Did anything happen during the course of the night? For example, did he get into any rows or fights? Receive any bad news or an upsetting phone call?'

'No. In fact, he was on good form and was chuffed that one of his closest mates was able to make it. He hadn't been sure if he was going to be able to get there.'

'Was that Steve or Bryan?'

'Bryan. Or whatever his name is.'

'How did Lloyd feel about moving back to the village and living here again? Did he have any concerns about it?'

'No, he wasn't worried at all. He said he'd done his time and was entitled to live wherever he wanted. His view was, if anyone had a problem with him, bring it on.'

'Since he was released, did he say anything to you about being followed or watched?'

'Yes, he did, and to Amy. He was certain of it. Even from his first night back on the outside.'

'Did he have any ideas about who it was?'

'He thought it was someone who was still upset about Joan's death. Or Dave.' He looked away and began banging mud off his boots.

If you had to guess, who would you say killed Lloyd?'

'I don't know. A lot of people had it in for him. The people who were annoyed with him over the speeding limit campaign. And the people who were understandably upset about Joan's death, but to go as far as murdering him? I can't see it.' He fixed his gaze on Sylvia. 'It takes a certain kind of person to kill, doesn't it?'

The words were out seemingly before he realised what he'd said.

Chapter 15

Ellie passed the village butcher's and spotted Nick in the shop. He had his back to the street and his arms around a chiller cabinet.

She knocked on the glass and went in. 'Don't usually see you in here on a Sunday morning.'

'We've got a new unit being delivered first thing tomorrow. I'm just getting this one ready to be taken away.' He wiped his hands and gave her a kind smile. 'I saw the newspaper article about Dave's arrest. I was going to call you actually, so I'm glad you popped in. How are you?'

'Not great. Dave's asked us to investigate. I wondered if I could ask you a couple of questions?'

'Sure. Let's go out the back. The sun's out.' He led Ellie up the step into a room with stainless steel worktops, fridges and freezers. 'I gather you had fun chasing about after Sophie's rabbit the other night.' He laughed. 'Carol and Jim are our pub quiz partners.'

Outside, the garden was mainly grass and brambles, but there was a small patio area. A black cat shot down the path and disappeared over the fence.

Ellie relayed her version of the Houdini story and they chuckled at the idea of two women on their hands and knees on the grass looking for a white rabbit while a man issued instructions.

'I feel sorry for Arthur,' said Nick, abruptly changing the subject. 'Poor chap. He's not long lost his missus. Now Lloyd. Must be an awful blow for him.'

'Yes, terrible.' She perched on a garden chair.

'How's Dave?'

'He's beside himself. Especially after Katie's article. Won't go out as he thinks everyone will stare at him.'

Nick swiped the air with his hand. 'I know it's not pleasant, but it'll blow over as soon as the police get the right guy.'

Ellie told him about the new police evidence and their investigation to clear Dave's name. 'I wanted to ask who had run-ins with Lloyd, either before Joan was killed or since he came out of prison? Just in case we've missed someone.'

Nick ran through all the people that Ellie already knew about. 'It wasn't just Lydia at the doctor's surgery. It was Dr Peters too. They're continually getting complaints over there from patients about the road, and how they've nearly got run over going into and coming out of the surgery.'

'I'd forgotten about him. Good shout, thanks. Yes, the practice is on the corner, isn't it? It's a bit of a blind spot too.'

Nick began fidgeting, pulling out weeds from around his feet and straightening the garden furniture. If Ellie hadn't known him better, she would have wondered if he was trying to signal he wanted her to go. 'There's something else though. You do know about Dave's history with Lloyd, don't you?'

She nodded. 'Sylvia said it's quite common for perpetrators to blame lead detectives for their punishments. I didn't know Lloyd had threatened to get revenge on Dave. It's very worrying.'

Nick was frowning. 'Is that all he told you?'

'Yeah. Why?'

'There's a bit more to it than that, Ells. Well, a lot actually. And it's to do with Dave's middle sister.'

'Hayley? Crikey. We haven't seen her in ages. What about her?'

'I don't want to be the one to tell you. You'll need to ask him about it.'

'Oh, OK, that sounds rather ominous.' She paused. 'I'll ask him when I get home.' She followed him back inside, muttering under her breath. 'Whatever it is, I wonder why he didn't he tell me. There's been a raft of revelations over the last twenty-four hours.'

'Sorry. It can't be easy. But you'll have to ask Dave.' He went to the fridge and took out a large beef bone for Rebus. Bagged it up and handed it to Ellie.

'Thank you. And for being a good friend all these years.'

He smiled warmly. 'Good luck. You're both my mates and I'd like to keep it that way.'

Chapter 16

Before Sylvia left Arthur's and forgot to do it, she texted Ellie, saying Lloyd had claimed to be scared Dave was going to kill him.

As she walked along the high street, her thoughts were busy. She refused to accept that Dave could have killed Lloyd, but if he had been threatening him, they all needed to know the details and context.

She passed the baker's. The smell of warm, spicy hot cross buns made her think of Ron. He'd always loved this time of year. On Easter Sunday, if he wasn't working, he'd make a special breakfast in bed for them both: pot of tea on a tray, cups and saucers – not mugs – jug of milk and a toasted, buttered hot cross bun each.

She arrived at the doctor's surgery. The flat above had its own entrance via a door to the left of the practice.

Sylvia rang the buzzer, hoping Lydia would be at home. She'd decided to only mention Dave being arrested if Lydia raised it.

The woman who opened the door had tortoiseshell glasses with round frames and hair tucked into a loose bun. A mauve cardigan lay on top of a purple polo neck jumper.

Sylvia introduced herself. She and Lydia had seen each other around the village several times but never said hello properly or been introduced. 'You left your gloves in a pew at church.' She held out a pair of lavender-coloured leather gloves, trying to get a read on the woman in front of her. She'd done a quick calculation on the walk over. Lydia was probably only five-ish years older than Ellie, but she looked about twenty years older. 'You're fond of the purple end of the colour spectrum then?' Sylvia smiled. Lydia reminded her a little of her mother. She had a similar absent-minded energy.

'Oh, *that's* where I left them. I'm such a n-n-n-nit-wit. My memory is shocking at the moment. Thank you.'

Sylvia had never noticed the stutter in the doctor's surgery. Perhaps it only happened in personal settings.

'I was helping to collect up the bibles and found them. One of the ladies said she was sure they were yours.'

'That was lucky.' Lydia patted her chest. 'Would you like to come in? I've just got back from a leg stretch with Barney. We were only going to stay here until I found somewhere else. Poor boy. A flat's far from ideal. Still, it means we get lots of exercise.'

'Thank you.' Sylvia entered a poorly-lit hallway with magnolia walls and a synthetic air freshener on a small table.

A chocolate Labrador came lolloping towards them, tail wagging, carrying a toy pheasant. His claws clacked on the old, sloping floorboards.

'And here's the man himself.'

Barney squeaked his toy, clearly used to being talked about as though he was human.

'The sermon was so apt this morning, wasn't it?' Lydia continued. 'About how d-d-d-difficult it can be to accept that people change.' She spoke quickly, as though she felt under pressure to say things. 'I rather forgot myself. Scuttled off afterwards because I wanted to write my thoughts in my journal before I forgot them.'

Sylvia gave her an understanding smile.

Lydia's facial muscles relaxed a little, creating a very different impression. 'So, you live in that splendid windmill.

Is it as lovely inside as it looks? I've been curious about that place since I was a child.'

'It's incredible. The light, space, acoustics. Only downsides are heating costs and cleani–' She stopped mid-word, realising, with her sleepless night, she'd forgotten to ask Ellie about the agency cleaner who'd last done Dave's flat.

'Everything OK?' asked Lydia.

'Fine, thanks. If you'll excuse me, I need to send a quick text.' She got out her phone, typed and sent the message, and returned her attention to Lloyd's sister. 'We were talking about the windmill.'

They chatted for a few minutes about the mill and Ellie's ancestors, who'd owned it for decades.

'I'm sure you've heard about my brother's death?' said Lydia, her voice jittery again. Her demeanour returned to how it had been when Sylvia arrived: troubled and anxious.

'Yes. My family and I are very sorry for your loss. It must be a terrible shock.'

'Well, yes and no. It's no secret that I disowned him after he ran poor Joan down. But I didn't expect anything like this to happen. None of us did.' Her eyes filled with tears. 'He should never have come back here. Amy and he should've gone somewhere else to live. Let everyone here get over what happened and heal.'

Sylvia had a feeling they were going to be hearing similar sentiments from other villagers in the coming days. 'Have the police spoken to you about your his death?'

She nodded. 'Oh, yes. Ian and I were amongst the first people they interviewed, I gather. I'm certain they think one of us killed him. Me, probably.'

'My husband was a detective. My son is one. It would be quite normal for them to speak to everyone who had a beef with Lloyd. I'm sure there's no cause for concern.'

'You say that, but I wouldn't mind betting, if they can't find the real murderer, someone will fit me up for it.'

Sylvia frowned, absorbing Lydia's strange remark. 'What makes you say that?'

She shrugged.

'Who do you think is going to fit you up? The police or someone else?'

'My brother.'

'But he's dead, Lydia.'

'I know that. One of his mates, I don't know. No doubt I sound completely paranoid, but he's been waiting to get back at me ever since he was charged with Joan's death.'

Sylvia followed Lydia along the hall into a small kitchen. It had a square table, with two chairs tucked under and a neat, red tablecloth.

'Do you have any idea who might have killed your brother?' Sylvia was bothered by Lydia's previous comments. Was it anxiety making her a bit paranoid, or did she know something she wasn't saying?

She shook her head. 'Apart from Dad, who will tell you *everyone* loved Lloyd, everybody else will say my brother unfortunately had a lot of enemies. Which is the truth.'

'Were you ever close?'

'No. He and I have always been chalk and cheese. As a boy, he could be cruel. Tormented the cat. And as a man, he was selfish. He took delight in provoking and antagonising people. Whereas I go out of my way to please.'

Sylvia caught flashes of embarrassment in Lydia's eyes.

'He rubbed a lot of local folk up the wrong way over the speed limit issue.'

'I remember,' said Sylvia. 'I wasn't living here in Wootton then, but I was in Deal. It was in all the newspapers and on the TV. My daughter-in-law's told me a few additional details.'

'Of course. Ellie knows most things that go on in this village. Partly instinct, I think, and her job.'

'True. Your father must be devastated about Lloyd. It sounds like he worshipped your brother.'

She nodded. 'Apart from a blip when Lloyd was in his late teens, he always did. In Dad's eyes, Lloyd could never do any wrong. When we had rows as kids, he always took Lloyd's side.'

'That must've been hard.'

'It was. Fortunately, Mum saw through it and picked Dad up on it. But it never changed his view. It just meant he and Mum had lots of rows.' She rolled her eyes and gave a minimising laugh.

'How do you get on with Amy? Ellie was telling me they went to school together.'

'She's a bit younger than me so I only really got to know her as my brother's girlfriend. He would bring her to parties and barbecues, that sort of thing. We got on OK. I never understood what she saw in him, but that was her business. I was concerned about her marrying him though.'

'What were you worried about?'

'That he'd cheat on her or hurt her. I never got the impression he took relationships seriously. He was regularly eying up other women, flirting, that sort of thing.'

'Didn't Amy notice?'

She shrugged. 'She must have but I got the impression she turned a blind eye.'

There was something here to explore further but Sylvia wasn't quite sure what it was.

'Did Amy ever share how she felt about Lloyd's campaign to get the speed limit lifted in the high street?'

'You're best off asking her about it really. She tried to make out she was neutral. She said she agreed with some of Lloyd's arguments *and* understood why people wanted a lower speed limit too.'

'Didn't you believe her?'

Lydia shuffled from one foot to the other. 'I did, sort of, but at the time I also suspected she didn't want to be honest with my brother. Now, however, I think she probably saw things from his point of view all along.'

'What made you change your mind?'

'She had ample opportunity to dump Lloyd, but she stuck by him. And even if she just wanted to support him while he was inside, she didn't have to get engaged to him.

She could've let him down gently or say she'd met someone else. But no. They got engaged relatively recently.'

'Oh?' She was reminded of Leonard's words about how much in love they were.

'Exactly. I realised she must genuinely have loved him. And I find that... well, intriguing, because Amy's not dim. And she knows what she wants. I ran into her at yoga the other day in the community centre. She gave me a big hug.' She frowned. 'But something very strange happened a couple of weeks ago.' Her demeanour clouded over.

'Oh?'

'I spotted Amy in the graveyard with another man. They seemed very familiar with one another and were talking animatedly. On the bench by the wall.'

'Did you get the impression anything romantic was going on between them?'

Lydia screwed up her face in contemplation. 'Oh no. Nothing like that. I assumed he was her brother or something.'

'Did you recognise him? Seen him before anywhere?'

'I'm not sure about that either. I definitely don't know him by name, but I couldn't rule out having seen him in the village before. Or the local area.'

Sylvia was looking forward to hearing what Ellie had made of Amy when she talked to her.

'Had you seen Lloyd at all since he was released?'

'No. Dad organised a "welcome home" party for him, but I said I didn't want to go.' She shrugged. 'I couldn't be hypocritical about it. I thought Lloyd should've got a much longer sentence for what he did. I didn't think he should come back here. And I wasn't going to be pleased to see him, so it seemed better for everyone if I stayed away. Dad and Amy were getting balloons and a banner for the front room and all that.' She shook her head. 'I couldn't get behind it. It seemed so disrespectful to Joan's poor family. You know? Everyone dancing around in paper hats with streamers and party poppers when the Chapmans are still desperately grieving the loss of their matriarch. It's all so inappropriate.' She closed her eyes and gently shook her head.

'I understand completely. It's got to be extremely hard for everyone.' Sylvia paused. She could only really ask a couple more questions without it being obvious she hadn't just come to return Lydia's gloves.

'Anyway – I understand they've got someone in custody now. That's what the new sergeant told me.'

Sylvia didn't want to say it was Dave and was keen to change the subject. 'Where do you think Lloyd was going on Saturday morning?'

'I honestly don't know. As I'd refused to go to the party, I've not been in the loop on family communication. Amy and Lloyd invited me to the wedding, and I'd had to say the same thing there: it was best if I didn't come.' She paused. 'He might've gone out for a dawn walk. Although I'm not sure my brother was really a dawn person. Unless he went fishing. Or – given he was getting married that day – maybe he'd been out for a few drinks the night before and didn't make it home? Got drunk and was killed on the way home.'

Both her comments were interesting. It was definitely odd that Lloyd had ended up in the pond. What had happened? Understandably, no details had been released to the public about the cause of death, but Sylvia remembered the picture wire they'd seen round his neck in Zoe's photos. And, if Lloyd's father knew Lloyd had been killed with picture wire, why didn't his sister?

'Before I go, do you mind if I check whether the police asked you where you were on Friday night or Saturday morning?'

'They did. I was at the Rectory, playing bridge. I partner Leonard sometimes. He's a much better player than me. We were playing some friends of Leonard's from his previous church in Harbledown. Got home around ten. Was asleep soon after and got up the usual time on Saturday morning. Around 9am.'

That was handy. She could check with Leonard. He'd mentioned he was playing bridge with friends, so it was most likely to be true, and she had no reason to suspect Lydia of lying anyway.

'Have the police said whether he was killed in the meadow or elsewhere?' So far, she'd learnt useful background information but not much that was new. It was too good an opportunity to miss getting an update from someone who'd talked to the police.

'In the meadow, they said, and pushed in the water after he was dead.'

Chapter 17

Ellie left Nick's shop with her mind churning. She took out her phone and dialled Dave's number.

He answered within a couple of rings, his voice full of gloom. 'Hey.'

'Are you at the windmill? I need to ask you about something.'

'I've just nipped out with Rebus. I can be back in five minutes or so. Is everything OK?'

'No. It's not. See you in a few minutes.' She rang Sylvia. She wasn't sure from what Nick said whether Sylvia knew about whatever had happened with Hayley, and there had been no point asking him. It was clear he didn't want to say, and that was fair enough.

'Ellie?' came Sylvia's voice down the line.

'Can you meet me at home in a few minutes? Nick's just told me some things that I need to discuss urgently with you and Dave.'

'Sure. I've just left Lydia's and was about to walk through the hare meadow to check something out, but I'll come home. I can do it another time.'

Ellie picked her way along the high street, past the poster advertising the village Bunny Hop the following Easter weekend, dodging lamp posts and containers of tulips and pansies. Avoiding people, and glances and comments – all while trying to gather her thoughts. To think through what Nick had just said so she could understand the implications.

Dave and Lloyd had history. They knew that.

But when Ellie mentioned Lloyd vowing revenge, Nick had said there was more to it than that, and it involved Hayley.

What the heck could he have meant? What could have gone on?

Immediately, crazy ideas darted through her mind. Had Hayley killed Lloyd? Was Dave protecting his little sister? Had Dave killed Lloyd to avenge his sister? No. Her imagination was running away with her. And she was realising Dave seemed to have a thing about protecting people.

Ten minutes later, when she let herself in, Dave was at the fridge, spooning yoghurt from the pot into his mouth.

Rebus hurtled to the door to greet Ellie, tail wagging like a propeller.

'Hey, boy.' She gave his ears a rub. 'Where are the kittens?' she asked Dave.

'All six are asleep for now. One of them got your phone charger, I'm afraid. It was on the desk in the office.'

Ellie didn't answer.

Sylvia followed her in and took off her coat.

Dave looked up. 'Right. What's up?'

She strode over to him. 'I asked you if there was anything else you hadn't told us and you said no.'

Dave frowned. 'What's this about?' He looked from Ellie to his mother.

'Don't ask me,' Sylvia said. 'I'm as much in the dark as you.'

'Tell me what happened with Hayley,' said Ellie. 'And Lloyd.'

'*Hayley?*' Sylvia's voice was full of alarm.

'And what it's got to do with Lloyd.'

Dave's eyes closed briefly in horror. He flicked the kettle on to boil. 'I'll get us a cuppa.' He gestured to the kitchen table.

Ellie sank down onto a chair, dread coursing through her. It again reminded her of when she found out about Dave's affair with Finn's mother, and she began to tremble. 'I don't like this,' she whispered. 'When you keep things from me. I hate secrets.'

Dave got three mugs out of the cupboard. 'Mum, I don't think you know this either.'

Sylvia frowned and joined Ellie at the table.

He focused on Ellie. 'The year you and Sally went to the States for summer camp – after our exams – Hayley started going out with Lloyd. She'd been going through a rebellious phase and been hanging out at the youth club in Deal. Started smoking and drinking. Nothing particularly abnormal except for the fact she developed a crush on Lloyd, and he seemed to see her as a bit of a coup, I think because she was a cop's daughter and my sister.'

He'd made their tea now and was at the table.

'And?'

He passed the steaming mugs over and sat down next to Ellie. 'For a couple of weeks, they were inseparable.

She talked about nothing but him. Lloyd this, Lloyd that. Lloyd says. You know what it's like.'

'She's younger than him, isn't she?'

'Yep. He'd started boxing, and got tattooed, and she would hang about, watching him train and fight. Very quickly, he told her he loved her. Hayley was seventeen but I'm pretty sure he was her first boyfriend, certainly the first serious one.'

'Oh, no,' Sylvia groaned. 'I don't like the sound of this.'

'Me neither. I sense a "but" coming...'

'That's because you know what he's like. Predictably, he got bored, and cheated on her.'

'Ugh. What a rat.' An idea popped into Ellie's mind. 'Not with Amy?'

'Yup. You guessed it. Hayley was staying with her best mate for the night, and Lloyd went to a party and got off with Amy in front of everyone. When Hayles found out, he said he was drunk–'

'He's been using that excuse for decades then.'

'– but he nevertheless dumped Hayley – who was heart-broken – and he started going out with Amy.' He heaved a deep sigh and let it out slowly, as though trying to control the pain the memory prompted. 'You know what first love is like. Hayley sat around for weeks, moping, waiting for him to call her or come round, to explain, to say he'd made a mistake and was sorry.'

'Did he?' asked Ellie.

'This is the thing. We all hoped he wouldn't. That she'd get over him. Start dating someone else. I kept introducing her to friends of mine who'd take her out – as a friend – and be kind to her. None of us wanted that scumbag Lloyd to come back into her life. But he did. Of course he did. He couldn't resist it.'

'What happened?'

'I came home from Nick's one evening and Lloyd and her were all cosy in her bedroom. Candles. Lying on bean bags, listening to Jeff Buckley. He'd climbed up onto our front porch roof, shinned up the drainpipe, and in through her window.'

Ellie gasped. 'For Hayley it must've seemed like a real Romeo and Juliet gesture.'

Dave nodded. 'Lying so-and-so. Told her he'd realised he loved her after all and that the thing with Amy had been a mistake. Begged her to take him back. Said he wasn't complete without her.'

'Oh, yuck.'

'Exactly. Anyway, when I saw them together, I lost it. Saw red and went for Lloyd. Punched him in the face. Hauled him off the bean bags, told him not to come near Hayley again and shoved him down the stairs.' Dave buried his face in his hands.

Ellie was holding her breath.

'Where was I?' asked Sylvia. 'I don't remember this.'

'Out at Bingo. You'd just been promoted at work and were celebrating with your colleagues. Dad was watching TV in the lounge. He had no idea Lloyd had sneaked in. He heard the shouts and came out. Took over from there. Bundled Lloyd into the car and took him home. Told Arthur what had been going on.'

Sylvia looked shocked. 'Why didn't your father tell me what had happened?' she asked.

'I don't really know, Mum.' Dave's eyes darted round the room. 'I think he didn't want to worry you.'

'You've got to be kidding, surely?' Sylvia stood up, face flashing with anger. 'That's the same ruddy excuse as you used earlier with Ellie. What is this rubbish about women not being able to cope with difficult situations? We're probably better at coping with them than men.'

'I... I... Maybe I got it wrong,' said Dave. 'It will have been how I remembered it at the time. I was only eighteen.'

Sylvia tutted. 'Don't you see? This is exactly how these patterns get passed on in families. Children see their parents behaving in a certain way and, without consciously realising it, they repeat the behaviour. You saw your dad do it and now you're doing it.'

Ellie could see the indignation on Dave's face.

'I did not. It was once, Mum. I can see you're upset but you're overreacting.'

'I'm not *overreacting*,' she snapped. 'My son hits someone and shoves them down the stairs and no-one tells me? What did your father say exactly?'

Dave took a deep breath. Looked at Ellie, then his mum. 'Do you really want to know?'

'*Yes*.'

'It was along the lines of, "We won't bother your mother with this. She's got enough on her plate at the moment with her job. We'll keep it to ourselves.".'

'Oh, great. It gets worse. Now I couldn't cope with my job. That's infuriating.' Sylvia stomped across the kitchen to the sink. 'See. You learnt that from him. Your dad. That women need to be protected from the truth. And you've used the same lame expression with Ellie.' She put her mug on the drainer. 'I can't take this in. I had no idea that Ron kept secrets from me.' She stormed over to the coat racks and flung her coat on. 'I don't know when I'll be back.'

With that, she flounced out, slamming the door.

Chapter 18

'Alright, I'm coming.' Arthur's weary voice made its way into the porch, making Sylvia suddenly regret coming round. But the door was open before she had time to change her mind.

'Fast asleep, I was,' Arthur said.

His glasses were halfway down his nose; hair tufts were sticking up, and his cardigan was on one side. 'Forgotten how uncomfortable that couch is.' He rubbed the back of his neck and groaned in pain.

'Sorry to bother you again,' said Sylvia. 'I've just found out about something that's knocked me for six, and wondered if I could talk to you about it.'

'To *me*?'

'If you don't mind. I won't be long.'

'I suppose. If you think it'll help.' His tone was matter of fact. 'You'd best come in.'

You've got to warn him. You can't just ambush him.

'It's to do with Lloyd and Dave.'

'Ah.' Arthur sucked in air through his teeth. 'We'll need tea then.' He led her along a dark hall, shuffling in his slippers and weaving round an assortment of things that seemed to have been dumped. An old bike, a fishing rod, a rucksack, an open toolbox.

Sylvia expected the kitchen to be similarly cluttered, but it wasn't, and looked as though someone had been having a tidy. She didn't know his family circumstances but, hopefully, he was getting help. A shiny brochure lay in the middle of the table. Sylvia recognised the colour and logo from when Ron had died. Wootton Funeral Directors.

'Do you need any h–?'

'I'll be alright. Thank you.'

He made them tea and took Sylvia into the conservatory where they sat on wicker furniture.

There was a large palm in a pot that was too small for it, an electric heater which wasn't plugged in, and a rack, stuffed with old newspapers.

Sylvia's nose picked up hints of paint and adhesive, and she got an unsettling sense of *déjà vu*.

'OK,' he said apprehensively. 'Fire away.'

'Dave's just told Ellie and me about Lloyd cheating on Hayley with Amy.' Her jaw was tight, and her cheek muscles were twitching disconcertingly.

Arthur nodded slowly.

'And Dave punching him,' she continued, 'and pushing him down the stairs. Ron never told me. And now he's dead, you're the only adult who was there.'

Arthur let out a heavy sigh. 'It was a long time ago.'

'Yes, it was. But it's been a shock finding out.'

He sipped his drink. 'It would be.'

'I can't understand why Ron didn't tell me.'

Arthur tapped his fingers on his mug. 'Perhaps he thought he was protecting you?'

'Argh. Not you as well with that "protection" nonsense.' She hadn't mean to be snappy.

Arthur frowned. 'Why nonsense?'

'Because I don't want anyone deciding for me what I should and shouldn't know. Particularly something like Dave shoving Lloyd down the stairs. He had to go to hospital.'

'It was a stupid scuffle. And I'm sorry you feel that way.'

'Did you and Ron discuss it at all?'

'Briefly.'

'Did *you* share what had happened with your wife?'

'I did not.' He paused, and Sylvia sensed he was deciding what to say. 'You're not going to like this but, since you're here and asking, I'll tell you. Ron and I agreed: the fewer people that knew about it, the better.'

Sylvia sat in her chair, almost frozen to the spot. Her emotions were bubbling up. But Arthur had just lost his son and she couldn't have a go at him over something Ron had agreed to years ago, even if they'd decided it together.

'I see,' she said in a quiet voice.

'Probably not what you want to hear but now you know.'

'No, but thanks for being honest. You've got enough to worry about. It was selfish of me to come round here, intruding on your grief.'

He gave her a sympathetic smile.

'I'm not good with secrets,' she said.

'None of us is.'

'It's like being on quicksand.' She surveyed the room while she gathered her thoughts.

Wooden blinds.

Two library books.

A clock that was face-down and without a battery.

On a tray, a collection of model aircraft caught Sylvia's eye. Some were bare wood; others were painted. Before she knew it, her thoughts had slid back to Ron. His interest had been in military models, but he'd loved building them too.

'I don't know why,' she whispered, 'and I don't like it, but I've got this awful feeling there's something else Ron's kept from me.'

Chapter 19

'That went well.' Dave groaned and closed his eyes for a few moments, then stared at the door his mum had just stomped through.

'It was inevitable,' said Ellie. 'She was never going to be happy that Ron kept this from her. I don't blame her, either.'

Dave shook his head. 'I guess. Except she wanted to know what happened and I'm not responsible for Dad's decisions.'

Ellie couldn't shift from her mind the knowledge that Dave had punched Lloyd and pushed him down the stairs; the image of him, so consumed with anger that he landed a blow on another human being, and shoved him, like a reviled object, down wooden stairs.

'You could've killed Lloyd. He could've broken his neck or his back.'

'It was a stupid hot-headed reaction. I wish I hadn't done it but that's pointless. I did. Thank goodness he wasn't too badly injured.'

Ellie hated violence. One of the reasons she'd fallen in love with Dave was that he'd never been that type of man. Or that's what she thought.

'I never had you down as someone capable of doing something like that. It's made me... I don't know. Wonder if I've really known you all this time.'

In her mind, she was picturing Lloyd turning up at Dave's flat, drunk and provoking him.

Dave was talking to her, but the words were a blur. Her thoughts were stuck in a groove and sliding fast. What if Lloyd had said horrible things about Hayley and Dave had lost his temper then too?

'Ells?'

'Oh, sorry. What?'

'What do you think I should do about Mum?'

'Er... she... she'll see you weren't responsible for what your dad decided to do. She's had a shock. And she's obviously disappointed–'

'In me.'

'In your dad, mainly. But in you a bit too for saying the same thing to *me* as your dad said about her.'

He let out a deep sigh. 'I don't like this, Ellie. I feel like everything is falling apart round me. My job, my career, my family. And I'm scared.'

'It'll pass. It's not nice, I understand that, but it will pass.' She gently massaged her temples where an ache had been developing. 'I've got some more questions, I'm afraid.'

Dave tensed.

'What's you punching Lloyd, and shoving him down the stairs, got to do with him going to prison and being released? There must be something you aren't telling me.'

'I'm coming to that. As I said, it was lucky Lloyd didn't hurt himself badly, tumbling down the stairs. He fractured a couple of ribs and had a black eye. His dad took him to hospital.'

Ellie was holding her breath. 'That's a serious injury.'

'It is. Back then, fortunately, it wasn't like things are now. I think his dad simply said he'd got into a scuffle. Something like that. If it had happened now, there would've been complaints. I'd have been reported to the police for assault and my life might've been very different. Who knows whether I'd have been able to go into the police.'

Ellie was reeling with shock. She understood Dave's anger at seeing Lloyd gaslighting Hayley, lying to her and trying to get her to take him back. But did that warrant violence? Did it make a difference that Dave had wanted to protect his little sister?

She wasn't sure how she felt, and that set off flutters of anxiety in her stomach and chest. 'Did Lloyd's mother know what had happened?'

'Not sure. I don't remember her being around or going to the hospital. Why?'

'And your dad didn't involve your mum. It's interesting, isn't it, that it's the men here who are covering things up and keeping secrets from the women. Ron, Arthur, you...'

Dave's eyes bulged with hurt.

'I'm not saying it to cause trouble. But given this situation has come up, and has echoes of the past, I think it's important that we talk about it. You can see how upset your mum is. *I'm* upset you lied to me about seeing Lloyd.'

'What do you want me to say, Ellie? I've said I'm sorry. I will think about it. I'll talk to Mum. We can all discuss it more. If I've got some psychological *thing* going on where I want to protect people I care about, I don't think that's necessarily bad.' He paused, his gaze shifting round the room. 'The issue is, as you pointed out, that people might not *want* protecting.'

'Hallelujah.'

'Particularly when it involves making decisions about what they know. However, can we please park all that for now and focus on solving this murder so I can get my career back?'

Ellie nodded, partly because she didn't have anything else to say.

'Thank goodness, Arthur wasn't that sort of parent and he let it go. Dad told him what had happened with Hayley. I think it helped that he was embarrassed about Lloyd's behaviour and said he didn't blame me for punching him.'

That was a surprise. Ellie would've thought Arthur would've made excuses for Lloyd. It wasn't important right now though. 'OK. But I still don't understand. How does all this relate to Lloyd being charged for killing Joan?'

'After what happened with Hayley, there's always been animosity between Lloyd and me. I never forgave him for how he behaved with her, and he's never forgiven me for punching him and pushing him down the stairs. I think we both decided – without discussing it – that we would never mention what had happened, to anyone. *He* didn't want people knowing how badly he'd treated Hayley, and *I* didn't want people knowing I'd lost my temper and had hit him.'

'That makes sense.'

'Ever since then we've stayed out of each other's way. It's not been easy but after a while, I got used to it. If I went somewhere and he was there, I'd leave, and he did the same. No big deal. We didn't have friends in common, so it wasn't a problem.'

Ellie knew exactly how it was. She'd done very much the same thing with Finn's mother, Andrea, after they'd fallen out in sixth form. And there were other people in the village who had ongoing feuds which they navigated.

'All came back up again though when he knocked Joan down on the crossing and I was put in charge of the police investigation. I was then in a position of power over him, and he made it clear he was not happy about that.'

'What do you mean?'

'He challenged everything I did. My competency. Said I wasn't treating him fairly and that I'd decided he was guilty before we'd even investigated.'

'But wasn't there indisputable evidence against him? Presumably he was breathalysed?'

'Yep. He was over the limit and there was ample CCTV evidence of him driving too fast, failing to brake and knocking Joan down. So, his complaints didn't really gain any traction, which was good for me in one way but unfortunately only served to wind him up more.'

'Ah, OK. Now we're getting there.'

'And he began threatening to tell everyone that I had attacked him and broken his ribs. His injuries had been logged on his medical records, so he *claimed* he'd have no problem proving assault. Although, whether records go back that far, I don't know. He might've been bluffing.'

'Oh, my goodness. That's awful. What did you do?'

'The first time he said it, I'll be honest, I panicked a bit. I had visions of being suspended, losing the job I love. All that. But I told myself it would be OK. I'd explain everything. We were teenagers. It wasn't going to jeopardise my career.'

'I'm sure it won't.'

'Anyway, when we put the evidence to the CPS for charging, we knew we'd get a conviction, so I basically made sure – as I always do anyway – that I did everything by the book: documented; recorded; witnessed, the lot.'

'Good.'

'He kept trying to get me alone with him. I wasn't taking any chances though. When it came to the court and sentencing, however, his lawyer advised him to plead guilty. Of course, Lloyd opted for that because he knew it would reduce his tariff. But his lawyer told him he stood no chance of an acquittal. Nevertheless, he *still* blamed his conviction on me and vowed revenge.'

'So, that's why he turned up at your flat. Do the police know about your fight with Lloyd over Hayley? If there's been bad feeling between you since sixth form, and Lloyd was threatening to go public about what happened, they could see that as giving you a motive to silence him.'

'I know. There's more, unfortunately.'

Ellie groaned loudly. 'Again?'

Dave ploughed on. 'That evening, when he came round, first of all, he started bragging about Hayley, commenting on her morals, her appearance, how easy she'd been to seduce. He said he knew where she was living and was going to see her. Have one last fling with her before he got married.'

'Unbelievable. So, he was goading you?'

Dave nodded. 'The guy was pond life.'

This was what Ellie had wondered about.

'I badly wanted to punch him again, Ells, I'm ashamed to say. It all came flooding back.'

'No, no, no.' She couldn't bear it. 'Please tell me you didn't...'

'Don't worry. I didn't. After the initial red mist, I remembered he and Amy were getting married and realised he was only saying it to wind me up. And Hayley's moved on, I think.' His expression changed. 'And he was on licence. So, theoretically, he needed to watch his behaviour.'

'Not that he seemed to care,' said Ellie.

'I know. Then he said he'd told Kent Police what I did to him. He told them I'd been threatening him, and he was scared of me. Scared for his life.'

'D'you think he did do that or was winding you up?'

'I don't know if he mentioned me punching him and shoving him down the stairs. I'm pretty sure he said I'd been threatening him. They asked me about it.'

'Have you?'

'If me telling him to get lost and not come round to my flat again is threatening him, then I did, but that's all I said. I laughed at him. Said I knew he was trying to wind me up, and, stupidly, said he'd have to do better than that.' He rolled his eyes, as though acknowledging his mistake. 'I'd just finished a long shift and a man had been killed at a junction by a reckless lorry driver and I wasn't in the mood to listen to his rubbish.' His voice caught on the last sentence and his eyes welled up.

Ellie swallowed. 'Surely you don't think he's behind the tread marks, the blood and the picture wire? He's dead.'

'No, I don't think that. But I'm sure he's been making allegations about me. Not in case he was murdered. That would be ridiculous. But to get me into trouble. They were serious with me, Ells. One phone call to the CPS from the chief inspector and I'd have been charged with murder. I still could be.'

Ellie shuddered. The Crown Prosecution Service were not to be taken lightly. 'One thing's certain. We need to find out who killed Lloyd before that happens.' She changed tack. 'How much does Amy know about this? Does she know what happened with Hayley?'

He shrugged. 'She's always refused to talk to me and acted like she's scared of me. I suspect one of two things happened. Either Lloyd told her some exaggerated version of the events, making me out to sound solely responsible and a complete thug... or he didn't tell her anything.'

'What's your hunch?'

'The latter. He's a coward.' He took a swig of tea. 'What she knows now though, I have no idea.'

Ellie let out a long sigh. 'This is awful. Who do you think killed Lloyd?' She got up and walked the length of the kitchen and back. Got a glass of cold water from the tap and drained it.

'I honestly don't know. He led such a messy life, there are so many people who hated him.'

'Enough to kill him though?'

'That's the tough part, isn't it? You know what it's like from Blix Investigators. People's motives often make sense to them but don't necessarily have an external logic. They get so fixated on whatever is eating them up, it becomes an obsession. At that point, real logic leaves the room.'

'Where is Hayley?' She looked at Dave who looked at her blankly.

'She was living in a campervan with her dog.'

'Great. Where?'

'I don't know. The last I heard, she was working on a fruit farm in the countryside outside Canterbury. Harbledown.'

Chapter 20

After the chat with Dave, Ellie took Rebus down to the beach to think about Dave's admissions. She parked the jeep on the seafront road and switched off the engine. Having received Sylvia's text about Dave's cleaner, she wanted to follow it up, so she got the agency's number from her contacts and dialled. They'd be closed but she could leave a message.

She listened to the greeting and spoke after the beep: 'Hi. Ellie Blix here from Blix Blitz. One of your staff members did a clean for me four days ago. Our client has a question he wants me to ask on his behalf.' She was trying to think what to say that wouldn't make the agency staff worry it was a complaint. 'It's about the alarm. Could you call me as soon as possible, please?' She conveyed the details and rang off.

She and Rebus got out of the jeep. The sky was like streaky bacon and the sea, a slate grey. On the shoreline, huge waves crashed onto the stones, the foam sliding in and out.

She crunched along the beach, her boots sinking in. Rebus had found a piece of wood that had washed up and was running about with it, smugly, like he'd found treasure.

Last time she'd walked along here, it had been with Zoe and Dave. Zoe had insisted on her dad giving her a piggy-back. She and Zoe hadn't known then that the man they loved had lost his temper, punched Lloyd Durden and pushed him down the stairs.

Rain spots started making their way down her collar and she shivered. She raised her hood, tucked her chin in and marched into the wind. Crunch, crunch, crunch on the stones. With each step she asked herself, did it matter? Did it make Dave a different person?

But no answers came back.

Next, she asked herself, did she think Dave had killed Lloyd? As Rebus charged back and forth on the beach, she walked down onto the sand. Again, she had no answer. She simply didn't know. It felt like the preoccupation was more: what if he *had* killed Lloyd? It was the same question she asked about everything. What if he had another affair? What if he hurt her again?

And how did she feel about him not telling her the truth?

As she sloshed through rock pools in her wellies, Rebus kept trying to make her throw his stick. He dumped it down near her, circled back, re-approached and nudged it forward with his nose, looking eager, whining and wagging his tail, then picked it up and started again – dumping it down. Wanting just one thing. No pretending, no concealing.

And then, just like that, he smelled a ball of fish eggs and suddenly the stick was abandoned, forgotten. All focus was on the empty, sponge-like egg sack, ripping chunks off it, dropping each one and letting it fly on the wind.

How much less complicated dogs were than human beings.

Perhaps, then, the issue with Dave not telling her the truth was trust, again. And, having been hurt, wanting guarantees.

Rebus tore up the last piece of fish egg, and Ellie assumed he'd return to his stick. But he didn't. Instead, he dropped onto his ear and shoulder, and folded over in a roll, grinding his back and rump into the sand in a gleeful gesture.

Ellie was sifting through other possible suspects when her phone vibrated in her pocket. She snatched it up, hoping it was Sylvia, but it wasn't. In her haste, she'd answered before seeing whose the number was.

'Ellie Blix speaking.'

It was Arthur, Lloyd's father. He explained he'd talked to Sylvia but couldn't get hold of her. 'Could she – or you – come round? It's urgent. I know who killed my son.'

'Sure.' Excitement reared up. This was quite the revelation.

'I'll leave the key in the door for you. I've overdone the digging. Got an ice pack on my knee.'

'D'you want me to come now?'

But he'd rung off.

That was odd.

Oh, well. She'd go straight round.

Ellie had never been to Lloyd's family home. She got the address from Sylvia and quickly collected Zoe so there would be a witness to anything he told them.

It was a yellow brick terraced house on a small 1970s housing estate. The first floor was covered with planks of grey clapboard. Some of the boarding was loose, and the roof was covered in moss. Paint was peeling off the window frames.

'Looks like the old boy has been struggling with the upkeep on his own,' said Zoe. 'I hope he's got heating.'

The key wasn't in the lock, but the door was ajar.

Ellie and Zoe entered the house. From within, a cheery presenter was talking away on the television.

'Arthur? It's Ellie Blix. Where are you?'

They walked in, Zoe closing the door behind them.

'Let's try the lounge,' said Ellie.

When they went in, Arthur was sitting on the sofa, motionless, eyes staring, his head back on the rest, a length of picture wire round his neck.

Beside him on the coffee table was an empty mug and a business card. Ellie recognised the Kent Police logo, and under it, Dave's CID contact details.

Ellie gasped and turned Zoe away from the dead body. She fished her phone from her pocket and dialled 999. 'Police, please.'

Chapter 21

Ellie was in the jeep, waiting for the police to speak to her about Arthur's death. Finn had collected Zoe and taken her home.

She dialled Dave's number.

He picked up on the first ring. 'Ells?' His voice was frantic. 'Where are you?'

'In the jeep. Any word from your mum?'

'No.'

'There's been–' Her voice broke. She sniffed and wiped her nose. 'There's been another death.' She told him about Arthur asking her to go round and see him. 'It's... I can't take it in. He said he knew who killed Lloyd.'

'No way.'

'But he rang off before I could tell him to call the police.'

'Oh crikey. Poor Arthur.'

'Garrotted.' She blew her nose and wiped the tears from her face with her fingers. 'Like his son.' She told him about the picture wire.

'I doubt that detail will have been released to the public, so it's got to be the same killer,' Dave replied. 'Far too much of a coincidence otherwise.'

'Suggests pre-meditation too. Whoever did it must've gone there to kill poor Arthur. Taken the picture wire with them.'

Rebus barked in the background.

'Sorry. Sarge has just arrived to do something with Mum's bees. Reeby wants to go out and say hello.'

For a brief moment, Ellie could picture it. Having just seen Arthur, dead on the sofa, she wished she was at home with them. Sarge working in the garden. The dog spinning round, whining and scratching at the back door.

'When Arthur rang you, did the number come up on your phone as his or as a different number?' asked Dave.

'I don't know.' She explained she'd answered without looking.

'Can you go into your call history and give me the number?'

'Sure.' She minimised the call screen and clicked on call history. 'Nope. Private number.'

'Hmm. That could mean a few things.'

'There's something else.' She told him about his business card being on the coffee table.

'That's very odd.'

'Would the new sergeant have given him one, do you think? Perhaps hers are being printed.'

'Doubt it. And she never asked me for some. So, if she was giving them out, she must've got hold of them without my consent. I can't ask her, for obvious reasons.'

'Might HR have given them to her? Or – I don't know how police systems work – your line manager?'

'Doubt that too. When I run out, I order more through our approved system. No-one else has my cards.'

'Well, someone's got hold of one. Have you never been round to Arthur's and given him your card? Recently or before Lloyd went to prison?'

'Definitely not since Lloyd was released. Did the card have a blue logo on it or a red one? They changed it a year ago.'

'Blue.'

'That's a new card. I bet the killer left it there deliberately to set me up. But I've no idea where they got it from.'

She asked again about Sylvia.

'I've rung her,' Dave replied. 'She's not answering. I left a message, apologising. Once she's calmed down, I'll have another chat to her. Are you still annoyed with me?'

'Yes. I am. And I don't blame your mum for being annoyed either. It's very unsettling when something happens, and people decide not to tell you, and you find out years later. Particularly when it's something big.'

'Mmm.'

'It feels like a real abuse of trust. You aren't consulted and other people decide what you should and shouldn't know. Ugh. Makes me furious just thinking about it.'

'I get that,' he said. 'Where do you think Mum might have gone?'

'It depends whether she wants to be alone or talk things through. She might just want company and no questions.'

'The cops have finished at my place so I can go back home, if that makes things easier. I don't want her to feel she can't return to the windmill because I'm there. It's her home.'

The two of them spoke for a couple more minutes and then rang off.

Ellie sat for a few moments, absorbing the conversation, enjoying the stillness and quiet.

Until a gentle, squawking meow broke the silence from the rear of the jeep.

'What on earth?'

Then another meow. And a tiny tabby kitten jumped up onto the back of the passenger seat, eyes shining.

'We have a stowaway, do we? Did you want to come with me so much, little one, that you sneaked into the jeep?'

And, tail erect and confident, the kitten dropped onto the seat next to Ellie and weed.

Chapter 22

Ellie hadn't been able to get hold of Sylvia since she stormed out of the windmill. She'd rung, left a voice message and had texted. It was fine if she wanted some space. Ellie simply wanted to check she was OK. She had never seen Sylvia as upset.

One place she hadn't tried was Mary's house.

Sylvia's mother lived in Sholden, and although it was only a mile or so out of Deal, it was sufficiently far to give a sense of distance, if that was what Sylvia wanted. And Mary wasn't the sort of person to ask prying questions. Her motto was to live and let live.

Ellie had tried Mary's landline a few times, but she rarely answered it and today was no exception.

Having returned the kitten to the windmill, Ellie was on her way to Sholden when her phone rang. The number on the SatNav screen was a mobile, not in her contacts. She accepted the call.

'Ellie Blix speaking,' she said into the Bluetooth mic.

'This is Emily from Kleanit. The boss has just picked up your message. We've got decorators in so she's at the office. You wanted to speak to me about an alarm?'

'Thanks so much for calling me back. You cleaned a ground floor flat at Goose Meadow in Lower Wootton on Wednesday.'

'That's right.'

'When you got the vacuum cleaner from the cupboard under the stairs, was there a pair of trainers in there?'

There was a pause. 'Yes. A white pair.'

She hoped Emily hadn't been following the news.

'And when you got the bleach from the cupboard under the sink, in the kitchen, was there a bag of picture wire and some cutters?'

'Not that I noticed. I had a few of the bottles out, not just the bleach, and I guess they could've slid down but he's pretty tidy. My manager said you were asking about the alarm too.'

'Oh, yes.' This hadn't been her area of interest, but she'd have to play along now. 'Was everything OK with it?'

'I told my manager as I wasn't sure whether it was the norm. The alarm wasn't on. Our policy is to leave properties as we find them, so, when I finished, I left the alarm off.'

'Oh. Right.'

'But because there was an alarm in place, and it didn't look broken, I reported it so the customer could be notified.'

'OK, thank you. I'll check with him.'

'Was everything OK with the clean? I'm not in trouble or anything, am I?'

'It was fine. He wasn't complaining. Simply wanted me to ask about the alarm. Thank you.' She double-checked she had Emily's number in case she needed it again, and rang off.

Five minutes later, she arrived at Mary's. She parked the jeep and got out.

In the front garden, several bags of bark were piled up on a rusty wheelbarrow next to a load of summer bulbs. The wisteria, which grew up the front of the house and trailed over the door and in between the ground and first floor windows, was sprouting leaves. The windows were sparkling in the March sun.

Ellie walked up the black and white tiled path. Someone had been weeding and cutting the lawn edges. Given Mary was in her eighties, it looked as though she'd either had paid help or had visitors recently.

Mary opened the door. She was wearing a long, swirly robe over shiny black trousers. Her white hair was piled on top of her head and held in place by a thick pin.

'Ellie, dear. How lovely to see you.' She gave her a warm smile. 'I'm making supper.'

Ellie explained there'd been a bit of a row with Dave, and that Sylvia had left.

'Oh golly. That doesn't sound good. Well, she's not here, I'm afraid. I wish she was. Hayley is staying for a few days. It's rather lovely actually.'

'*Hayley*? What's she doing here?'

'I don't really know. She arrived the other day.' She glanced over her shoulder and dropped her voice. 'But *something's happened,'* she whispered. 'No idea what but she's terribly upset.'

Chapter 23

'Hayley? Oh, my goodness, how are you?' Ellie blurted.

She wasn't sure, from the way Dave had spoken about his sister, whether they were on good terms still. If they weren't, it wouldn't make it easy to talk to Hayley. 'I was trying to think when we last saw each other.'

Dave's younger sister heaved in a breath and zipped up her hoodie. 'Was it at Zoe's eighteenth birthday party? I drove over from Barcelona in the van.' Her brown hair was pulled back into a messy ponytail with strands at the front and sides framing her face. Ellie had forgotten how much like Dave she looked.

'Does your mum know you're back?' Sylvia and Dave couldn't know, surely, or they'd have mentioned it.

They were in Mary's kitchen, a double room which had been knocked through into a welcoming open plan space.

Hayley shook her head. 'Not yet. I haven't felt like talking to anyone. I lost Meg a couple of weeks ago and the van broke down in northern France.' Her eyes welled up. 'I can't get used to waking up and not seeing a large black and white lump on the bed first thing, and dog hair everywhere.'

'So sorry. She was such a precious girl. Typically collie in so many ways, and unlike one in others. I always remember her and Reeby playing in the stream in Appledown Woods. Must've been a few years ago.'

Hayley forced a tight smile.

'I guess you've not been in touch with Dave then, either? Or Karen?'

Karen was the youngest sibling.

Hayley shook her head.

'Last I heard, you were in Harbledown,' said Ellie.

'That was a couple of years ago. From there I went over to Europe.'

Mary joined them, carrying a vase of spring flowers and aromatic branches from the garden.

'Mmm. Eucalyptus and rosemary,' Ellie said, inhaling their pungent smell.

'I've not been in touch with Dave for a while,' Hayley replied. 'I knew you two had split up. Which I was very sad about. Are you still–'

'Separated. But good friends.' She flickered a smile. 'If that doesn't sound a cliché.'

'Not at all. I'm sure there are lots of people who are separated and *aren't* good friends.' She tucked her hair behind her ears. 'Anyway, what brings you round to Gran's?'

Ellie caught the nervousness in Hayley's question. She explained about Sylvia and Dave's row. 'That's not it though, I'm afraid. Dave is in trouble.'

'What sort of trouble?' asked Hayley. 'He hasn't been losing his temper again and getting into fights, has he?' She let out a weak laugh, the way people sometimes do when they're trying to pretend that something serious is a joke.

Ellie stared at her. 'What d'you mean?'

Hayley forced a hollow laugh. 'Oh, forget it. I was just joking.'

'You weren't though, were you? What did you mean?' Did Hayley know something they didn't?

This case was like a maze. They kept finding themselves going round in circles and up dead ends.

Hayley sat twiddling her hair.

'I assume you know about the man who was killed a couple of days ago?' Ellie asked eventually. Did Hayley know Lloyd was dead? Ellie was finding the conversation a bit surreal.

'*I've* been following it on the news,' said Mary. 'Lloyd Durden.'

Hayley's face drained of colour, and she swayed on her feet, grabbing hold of the dresser to steady herself.

'Are you OK?' Ellie went over to her. 'Do you want to sit down?' She pulled a chair out from the table.

'He's the thug that ran over Joan on her crossing,' said Mary, her attention on the branches she was arranging and apparently oblivious to her granddaughter's reaction. 'A bit odd he's released from prison and ends up dead a couple of weeks later.'

Hayley sank down onto an upholstered seat and perched, hunched over, her eyes closed. Her frame was gaunt and thin, not the fit, muscley Hayley Ellie remembered.

Questions were darting through Ellie's mind. 'Shall I make you a cuppa? Or get you some water?'

'Please,' replied Hayley, her voice barely audible. 'Either.'

'Let me do that,' said Mary as she filled the kettle and put it on the Aga to boil.

'Did you know about Lloyd's death?' she asked Hayley, keeping her voice gentle.

She nodded.

'Did you know him, child?' asked Mary, suddenly seeming to switch onto what was going on. 'This awful *Lloyd creature*?'

'Er... a bit, Gran. From school.' She fixed her gaze on Ellie's face, as though searching for clues as to what she knew.

Mary's question suggested she and Hayley hadn't discussed Lloyd. By name, at least.

'He was getting married,' Mary continued. 'The day he was killed. To one of the veterinary nurses at the local practice. Lovely girl. Amy Hardcastle. Such a romantic name. Sounds like the heroine of an Agatha Christie novel.'

'Excuse me. I don't feel–' Hayley rose to her feet and dashed out of the room.

'She's not herself at the moment,' Mary whispered. 'Been up and down like a yo-yo. Happy one minute, angry and tearful the next. I haven't wanted to pry.'

'I'll go and see if she's OK.'

'I've just heard the patio doors open so she's probably in the garden. It's where she's spent most of the time since she got here.'

Ellie gave what she hoped was a reassuring smile. 'No problem. Could you try and get hold of Sylvia?'

Outside, Ellie made her way down the path in Mary's garden, trying to figure out what was best to say to Hayley. She was clearly upset, and it seemed as though the mention of Lloyd had stirred her up.

Ellie felt like she was wading around in treacle, not really knowing what was going on. She couldn't understand why Hayley would be *so* distressed by Lloyd's death. Was there something else they didn't know? Had something happened in the interim years?

Movement in the summer house caught her eye. The lamp was a warm glow in the window.

'Is it OK to come in?' Ellie asked, popping her head round the wooden door.

Hayley nodded.

Ellie sat down on a wicker chair. 'You said you already knew about Lloyd's death, yet you also seemed really shocked when Mary mentioned his name. Why?'

'Not shocked so much as it brought everything back.'

What was 'everything'?

'You didn't keep in contact with him though, did you? After school, I mean?'

She let out a pained sigh. 'Every so often I'd get a message from him, asking how I was. Either through Facebook or by text. I kept blocking him and he'd reappear using a new account or phone number.'

'Did you tell him to stop?' It felt a bit too close to stalking.

'Each time.'

'Why did you think he was getting in touch?'

'Certainly not because he was genuinely concerned how I was. As always with him, I'm quite sure he simply wanted to know whether I'd forgotten about him, whether the door was still open, if you know what I mean.'

Ellie nodded.

'Pathetic and narcissistic.'

'And unkind,' said Ellie. 'I'm sorry. That must have been very painful for you. It's difficult to move on when someone won't leave you alone. Very selfish of him.'

'Do the...' Hayley began another sentence and hesitated. 'Do the cops really think Dave killed him?'

'We don't know.' She told Hayley about the arrest and release. Dave's "gardening leave". The alleged threats. The trainers and picture wire. The row with Sylvia.

'Oh dear. What a mess.'

Although the words sounded sympathetic, the way Hayley said them suggested she felt conflicted. Ellie was finding it difficult to gauge where her sister-in-law was at emotionally. Surely, she didn't still have feelings for Lloyd?

Ellie also had questions about the timing of Hayley's return and what exactly had prompted it. She'd mentioned the dog dying. Was that the reason? Where did the demise of the camper van come into things? Had she been on her way home when it conked out, or had there been another catalyst?

'I'll give Mum a ring,' said Hayley. 'Arrange to meet up with her. After all, it was me they rowed about.'

'I'm sure she'll be pleased to hear from you. It wasn't you really.' Ellie tried to phrase the next sentence carefully. 'It was more that your dad didn't tell your mum about Lloyd cheating on you, and about Dave losing his temper with him.'

'Ah. So, you know.'

'Yes. I won't say who, but someone said there was more to the animosity between Lloyd and Dave, and that it involved *you*. Your brother eventually filled us in.'

Hayley was studying her fingers.

'Going back to your mum, I think it annoyed her more because something similar happened with Dave and me very recently. He didn't tell me that Lloyd had been round to see him.'

'I see,' said Hayley. 'You won't hear me defending Dave over that incident when we were young, but it wasn't his fault that Dad didn't tell her. It was Dad's decision.'

'I know.' Ellie was absorbing Hayley's response. 'But it was Dave's choice not to tell me Lloyd had been round last week, and I think your mum's anger got mixed up with that. I can see how that happened.' She gathered her thoughts. 'Can we rewind a moment? Back there, you mentioned Dave "losing his temper and getting into fights". Were you referring to the fact he punched Lloyd and shoved him down the stairs, or something more... I don't know... generalised? Or more recent?' She paused, concerned Hayley might walk off again. 'A few people have said Lloyd claimed Dave was threatening him, and that he was scared Dave was going to kill him.'

'Well,' Hayley shrugged dismissively, as though vindicated in her remark, 'there you are. Wouldn't surprise me one bit. Dave's always been obsessed with Lloyd.'

Ellie still didn't catch Hayley's drift. She was also wondering about Hayley's 'you won't hear me defending Dave' comment.

'What do you mean? Are you saying you think Dave killed Lloyd? Are you suggesting Dave was violent a lot when we were growing up?'

Hayley looked away.

'I'm finding it hard to pinpoint what you're implying and it's important,' Ellie continued. 'Dave's in a lot of trouble. And Lloyd is dead.'

'He was like a dog with a bone.' Hayley's head was raised, tilted back and her jaw jutted forward. 'Always going off at Lloyd. It became an obsession for him.'

'Did you talk to him about it?'

She snorted. 'Ha, yeah. Tried that. He wasn't interested. Thought he knew best, just like he still does.'

Hayley was angry. That was obvious. But what about?

'It's still possible for you two to discuss it. Put the past to rest. I'm sure he'll say he thought he was protecting you. No?'

'Course he will. Just like he did then.' She stared at Ellie, narrowing her eyes. 'But I didn't want his "protection". I loved Lloyd. Dave ruined everything.'

So, that was it. She blamed Dave for her relationship ending with Lloyd.

Ellie sensed she was only going to get so far with Hayley. This was going to be one of those situations where it would take a while, and several discussions, to tease out what happened and what everyone felt. And it involved more people than the two of them.

'What's brought you back, Hayles? Are you home for good?'

'I...' Hayley broke off. 'Everything's gone wrong again.' She let out a sob and pulled a tissue from her pocket. 'I thought I'd...' she said through tears, 'dealt with things... Got over it all ... and moved on. But I haven't... When I said hearing Lloyd's name brought everything back... that's what I meant.'

'Brought *what* back exactly? D'you mean Lloyd cheating on you? Or Dave punching him? The relationship finishing?'

'Those things too. But I was talking about the baby. *My* baby. This wasn't how it was meant to be.'

Chapter 24

As Ellie drove home, her head was spinning with questions about Hayley's baby, and about Dave's fight with Lloyd. Although it had happened a long time ago, it was news. Who had known about it all?

She'd promised Hayley she wouldn't tell anyone about the pregnancy for a day or so, as long as Hayley told Sylvia and Dave as soon as possible, and the police straightaway, in case they might consider it gave Hayley a motive to kill Lloyd.

The other thing Ellie couldn't shake from her mind was what Hayley had said about Dave losing his temper and getting into fights. How easily she'd considered her brother capable of killing Lloyd. They needed to talk more to her about this.

The back roads between Sholden and Lower Wootton seemed dark. All she could think about was the long hot bath she was going to have when she got in. Candles. Dressing gown warming on the radiator. Perhaps even a glass of wine. She'd been bombarded with new information all day. She'd happily never speak to anyone again.

But when she opened the front door, dance music was thudding from the lounge, and the mouth-watering smell of a roasting chicken reached her. The oven light was on, and Dave was at the kitchen table, on the phone.

Her heart sank.

He mouthed 'hi'.

Zoe and Finn were in the lounge. Zoe lay on her back on one sofa with a paperback, and two kittens asleep on her legs. Finn was on the other sofa, cross-legged, playing with his phone, a kitten on his shoulder, pawing at his hair.

'Gran's upstairs,' said Zoe.

For a moment, Ellie felt like she'd been transported back in time to before she and Dave split up. Although Finn and Sylvia wouldn't have been at the windmill; but the atmosphere, the family gathering, it prompted a tugging combination of joy, melancholy, fear and longing; strange feelings, ones she'd not felt for a while.

Uppermost, though, was irritation. She badly wanted some time alone where she didn't have to think about other people's feelings and keep checking what she said. Dave, Sylvia, Hayley. She loved them all, but she just wanted to be on her own.

'Dad's cooking a roast,' Zoe announced. 'Whether it'll be edible or not remains to be seen.'

In the time they'd been separated, Dave had often popped round. She'd get home and he was mending Zoe's bike in the garden with Finn or putting up a shelf for Zoe in her bedroom. But in that whole period, she had never got home and found Dave cooking a roast. It wasn't an unpleasant idea necessarily. She was tired and hungry and hadn't given a thought to supper. But it was the closest they'd ever been to a 'couple' scenario.

And they weren't a couple.

Did it matter?

She wasn't sure. It wasn't just that she wanted a bath. Something about it bothered her but she couldn't put her finger on which bit.

Ellie went through and sat down next to Finn.

'Sylvia's invited the vicar,' Finn said.

'Great. Another person. Who's Dave on the phone to?'

'His union rep, I believe.'

'Have there been developments?'

He shrugged. 'Best you ask Zo. He's worried he's going to be sacked. Something to do with his age and pensions, and the chief super.'

Chapter 25
MONDAY

The following morning, Ellie woke up with a stiff neck, having had a kitten tucked under her chin all night. She'd slept badly, intermittently dreaming about Hayley's baby and lying awake, fretting about keeping the news from Dave. She'd been angry with him for keeping things from her, and now she was doing the same.

The night before, when she got back to the windmill, she'd wolfed Dave's roast and escaped as quickly as she could to the pet shop flat for a bath in peace. Guilt had gnawed at her all evening, especially given the super was now muttering to Dave about early retirement.

A meow brought her back to the present.

She bundled the kittens back into the jeep, drove home to the windmill, checked the Blix Blitz diary and walked Rebus...

All by 9am.

After poor sleep and a couple of coffees in quick succession, she was like a whirling dervish. She'd crash later, for sure.

Her next task was to visit Amy. There were several things Ellie wanted to ask her. The difficulty was they were all extremely sensitive topics, and she had to assume Amy would know – either via the village grapevine or the newspaper – that Dave had been arrested and she might not want to talk to Ellie. She'd therefore decided on one key question: who was the man Lydia saw her with in the graveyard?

Having chewed on it ever since she woke up, Ellie decided all she could do was to call round to Amy's and play it by ear. Thank goodness they'd always got on OK at school. They hadn't known each other well back then, but they also hadn't had the opportunity to fall out in the way that girls so often did. That might enable her to say that Dave had been released and wasn't guilty.

Amy's flat was on the high street, above the dentist's, in the same area as the pet shop and the doctor's surgery.

A woman Sylvia's age opened the door to Ellie, presumably Amy's mum. She was familiar from the village.

'Hi. I've come to see Amy.'

'Well, if it isn't Dave Blix's missus,' the woman said. She was dressed in dark jeans and a red jumper. 'I doubt very much she'll want to talk to you.'

'What the heck is *she* doing here?' screamed a voice from the lounge.

Ellie's phone vibrated in her pocket and a text message pinged.

The television got louder as a door opened. Footsteps on the stairs.

Ellie heard Amy before she came into view. 'You've got some nerve on you.' Amy was in the hall now, eyes flashing with anger, her dressing gown undone. 'Being all friendly to me at yoga. Buying me a coffee and asking me questions. And all the time your husband was down at the nick, under arrest for murdering *my fiancé*.'

Ellie swallowed. She couldn't really deny either accusation. Might she be able to explain?

'I was genuinely pleased to see you and was worried about you.' She tried to keep her voice steady and low. 'I'm sorry if my questions seemed out of order. I can't even remember what I asked.'

'We were meant to be on our honeymoon now,' Amy spluttered, tears coursing down her face. 'Planning the rest of our lives together. Instead, I've got to list my wedding dress on eBay and organise a funeral.'

Ellie gulped.

'You should've told me Dave had been arrested. Not walked home with me, pretending to be my friend.'

'I wasn't pretending. I wanted to make sure you got home OK and that you'd got something in your stomach.' She took a deep breath. 'I didn't tell you because I–' She broke off, realising she was about to say, 'I didn't want to upset you.' She almost turned and ran in shame. 'I'm really sorry. Dave was released within a few hours, and he did not kill–'

'Get out of it.' Amy swiped the air with her arm. 'I'm not interested in your excuses. And if you've come round here hoping I'll give you information to help you get your murdering husband off the hook, you can think again.' She barged past Ellie and thundered out of the flat in her dressing gown, slamming the front door behind her.

'Murdering husband' echoed in Ellie's ears. She swayed and grabbed hold of the bannisters, her head throbbing. It was as though the hall walls were leaning in. Her legs collapsed beneath her, like a broken umbrella, and she slid to the floor with a thud.

'Are you OK?' a voice asked.

She looked up. Amy's mother was standing over her.

'Could you give me a minute? I...'

Her phone vibrated again and pinged.

'Stay there. I'll get you a glass of water.'

A few minutes later, Amy's mother was back. She handed Ellie a glass. 'Have a sip of that. Take deep breaths.'

'I shouldn't have come. It was silly of me. I...'

'He's been released, you say, your husband?'

Ellie nodded and sipped the water.

'Come and sit in the lounge for a minute. It's hard on the floorboards, and there's a draught from the door.' She took hold of Ellie's arm and helped her to her feet, steering her up the steps into the lounge.

It was a warm, welcoming room, painted white with the chimney breast a deep, Victorian red. The carpet was cream; thick and spongy beneath her shoes. For a moment, Ellie wished she could lie down and close her eyes.

She perched on an armchair. This case was getting to her. It was always upsetting, asking friends and neighbours questions when people were murdered, but the revelations about Dave – and his arrest – made it all so much more complicated.

'Thank you. Sorry. I'll go in a minute,' Ellie burbled. She felt like she had to keep talking. 'I'm house sitting at the pet shop for a few days.' Once she started, she found she couldn't stop. 'Well, pet sitting, really. The owner's cat had kittens a few weeks ago and she had to go away at short notice, so I'm looking after them. Gorgeous little tabbies, they are.' What was she doing? Why was she telling Amy's mother all this?

'Ah, Tabitha. We've got one from her first litter.' Amy's mother pointed to the bundle of fur asleep on the sofa. 'Amy helped with their injections and asked for one.'

After a night of broken sleep and bad dreams, Ellie was getting her bearings. 'I'm sorry about making Amy feel worse.'

Her phone vibrated a third time. Someone wanted her.

'She's feeling very raw at the moment. Understandably. It's going to take time. Arthur and I have been trying to talk to her about the funeral, but she's refused to discuss it.'

This gave Ellie an idea. 'Could her brother help out with that?'

Amy's mum frowned. 'She doesn't have a brother. It's just Amy, her sister and me.'

'Oh, sorry. I don't know where I got that from. I saw her with a man in the graveyard. I assumed he was her brother... or family.'

An imperceptible look shot across the woman's face.

'I was walking the dog,' Ellie continued. 'Last week, was it? I lose track of the days. The two of them were sitting on one of the benches together by the wall at the back by the compost heap.' This obviously wasn't true. It had been Lydia who'd seen Amy. Ellie said *she* had so Amy's mother couldn't just say Lydia had got it wrong and change the subject.

'You'll have to ask her about that. I don't know anything about it.'

'I thought he looked familiar,' Ellie continued. 'Anyway – it doesn't matter.'

'I hope no-one else saw them.' Amy's mother was frowning, seemingly unable to let the scene recede in her mind. 'You know what villages are like for gossip.'

'I don't know. I suppose anyone walking through the graveyard, or along the footpath beside the church, might have seen them.' Ellie deliberately made the scenario easy for Amy's mum to visualise in case she had any comments.

She felt a stab of guilt for being deceitful and changed the subject. 'Have the police found out who was following Lloyd, do you know?'

'Not that I've heard.'

'It must've been scary for him. How long had it been going on for?'

'Now that I *do* know. Ever since he came out of prison. Literally the first night. He came here with Amy and popped to the bistro in the village to get us pizzas for tea, and some wine from the off-licence, and he was convinced someone followed him home.'

Chapter 26

'The alarm was off when the cleaner arrived?' said Dave. 'And she left it off when she'd finished?'

He and Ellie were in his Audi on their way to the Rectory.

She had just told Dave what Emily had said. 'Sorry. I was so tired, I completely forgot to tell you last night.'

'It's never off, except when I'm at home. What day was this? Was I definitely not in?'

'No. I double checked. She assumed you might have been because of the alarm.'

Ellie gave him the day and time.

'That's correct. I was out all day Wednesday. But when I got home around 6pm, the alarm was back on. How the heck can that have happened?' He flicked the indicator to pull into the road by the vicarage. 'Might the cleaner have gone back to put it on?'

Ellie repeated what Emily had said about leaving properties as they found them. 'I suspect once she'd informed the agency the alarm was off, she moved onto her next job.'

'And they didn't inform you, this Kleanit outfit? You were their customer.'

'Nope. I shall be having words. But back to your alarm… Might the police have returned to your flat for something?'

'Not without permission. I reckon someone's been in. I suspected as much when the blood and picture wire miraculously appeared. Now I'm sure of it.'

Ellie's phone rang. It was Zoe.

'Hi, lovey,' said Ellie. She'd been at Amy's when Zoe had been calling. 'Everything OK?'

'It's Sophie,' Zoe screeched down the phone. 'She had a gig last night and hasn't come home. And she's not answering her phone. It goes straight to voicemail.'

Ellie switched her mobile onto loudspeaker so Dave could hear.

'Talk to your dad. He's here.'

They'd arrived at the vicarage now.

Dave switched off the Audi's engine. 'Here's what I want you to do.' He talked Zoe through a set of instructions, made sure she was OK and rang off.

'I'd better text Fran,' said Ellie. 'Give her the heads-up about Sophie, otherwise it'll be a shock if she gets a call from the police.'

'And I'll ping the chief inspector a text in case Zoe forgets to ring the police,' said Dave.

They both sent their messages and put their phones away.

'Right.' Dave turned to Ellie. 'Do we think Mum's here with the vicar?'

Chapter 27

The Rectory was an eighteenth-century brick and flint building with a gravel drive and ivy trailing up the front.

'She's not at her mum's,' said Ellie, 'so I reckon she's here with Leonard.'

'D'you think he and Mum might have a future?' Dave undid his seatbelt. 'They clearly get on well together. And I couldn't help noticing that she was putting on her lipstick and earrings to go to church.'

Ellie chuckled. 'And dyeing her hair. Zoe and I spotted that a few weeks ago. I don't know though. I get the feeling she's still getting over your dad's death. I think it's partly why it's stirred her up, learning something about him that she didn't know.'

'Ah. I see. I hadn't realised that. I thought she was doing OK.'

'She is. But these things take time, don't they?'

The windows were starting to steam up.

He nodded. 'You were always closer to her than me.'

'That's not true. Sylvia and I are close, but our relationship is less complicated. She's not my mum and there's nothing tricky lurking about in the background. Apart from you cheating on me, but she's always been very good at keeping whatever she thought and felt about that out of our interactions. Even when I was upset, she was careful not to take sides.'

'Oh, come on. She was always on your side.'

'I'm not sure that's true. She's extremely fond of you. And cares immensely. Don't underestimate that.'

'So, basically I've got to eat humble pie.'

'Not necessarily. She'll realise – if she hasn't already – that you're not responsible for your dad not telling her you lost your temper with Lloyd. But if you keep saying it wasn't your fault, and she's still annoyed, it's harder for her to let go. If it were me, I'd simply keep reiterating that I'm sorry.'

'What would I do without you?'

She shook her head vigorously. 'Let's not go there again. I'm not responsible for you, and you aren't responsible for me. OK? I'm happy to help where I can, but when you don't tell me the truth, I don't want to.'

'Fair enough. C'mon, let's go and see if Mum's here.' He went to open the door.

'Hold on.' She put her hand on his arm. 'When we go in, there's something I need to tell the two of you.'

'Oh? Should I be worried?'

'That's trying to pre-empt what it is. You'll know shortly, along with your mum.'

They got out and walked up the path.

Leonard opened the door. 'Ellie. Detective Inspector Blix. Are you looking for Sylvia?'

'We are,' said Dave. 'Is she here?'

'She is. Do come in, won't you? She's been rather upset so I'm sure she'll be pleased to see you.'

He led them along a wide hallway into the lounge where a jigsaw puzzle was laid out on a bridge table, an image of Deal Castle forming from the pieces. Sylvia sat at one end, and opposite her, there was an empty chair.

'We were worried about you,' said Ellie. 'You weren't at your mum's so this was the only other place we could think of.' Ellie deliberately didn't mention Hayley being at Mary's house. They could discuss that later.

'Should I go and make us some tea?' said Leonard. 'I've got a rather nice banana and toffee cake cooling on the rack, if you'd like a slice of that.'

'That sounds lovely, Leonard, thank you,' said Ellie, pleased to be able to talk to Sylvia alone.

'You alright, Mum?' said Dave. 'I'm so sorry I upset you, blurting out stuff about Dad from years back.'

Leonard left them. Ellie got the impression he'd been lingering to check Sylvia was alright.

'I should have been more considerate.' Dave sat down in the seat opposite Sylvia. 'Terrific picture of the castle on that puzzle. I've seen a couple of pieces already. Can I put them in place?' His face lit up and he looked like he was itching to get going.

Ellie remembered how much he'd enjoyed doing puzzles with his mum when they were kids.

'Go ahead,' replied Sylvia.

'Did you know Arthur's been killed?' Ellie said to Sylvia. 'He asked us to go round and see him but was dead by the time we got there. Poor man.'

'No! That's terrible.'

'Same method,' said Dave. 'Garrotted with a picture wire.'

Ellie told her about Dave's business card being left in Arthur's house.

'Is someone trying to set you up?' asked Sylvia.

Ellie glanced at Dave, keen to hear his reply.

'It's the only thing that makes any sense,' he replied. 'Too much of this is, as yet, unexplained. With Arthur's death now too, we need your help, Mum. Please come home. I'm really sorry I upset you. It wasn't my intention at all.'

Sylvia cleared her throat. 'It's OK. It was unfortunate timing. You'd only just admitted to not telling Ellie the truth about seeing Lloyd, and then you let on that your dad hadn't told me the truth either.' She paused and drew breath. 'The actions themselves were bad enough. What finished me off was that both you and your dad trotted out the same sexist excuse.'

Dave looked down at his hands, turning them over and examining his nails. 'I get that. And it hadn't really occurred to me it was sexist. So, it's been quite enlightening.' He scratched his stubbly chin. 'I've never seen myself in those terms, but it's made me wonder if I do say things that are sexist.'

'I can't say I've seen you that way,' said Ellie, 'either when we were kids or as adults.'

Dave smiled appreciatively.

Leonard arrived, carrying a tray of tea things. Teapot, cups and saucers, cutlery and plates, a sweet-smelling loaf cake on a stand.

'Thing is, you and your dad aren't the only ones who used that expression. Arthur did *and* Leonard.'

'Got a proper telling off for it too,' Leonard explained.

'Never mind,' said Sylvia. 'We talked about it, and I apologised for getting huffy.' She told them about her last conversation with Arthur.

'So, his wife never got to know about my fight with Lloyd either?' said Dave.

'No,' replied Sylvia. 'You know, I've been wondering if I've been a bit harsh on your father. He was older than me after all. Perhaps it was more normal for men then to make decisions on their own...?'

'Who wants tea?' said Leonard jovially. 'Shall I pour?'

Ellie chuckled. Leonard's diplomacy skills were excellent.

'Wow,' said Dave. 'Look at this spread. We'll have to come here again. I'm usually at work. Lucky if I can get a KitKat from the vending machine.'

'I understand you're on gardening leave,' said Leonard. 'Sylvia told me. Any progress?'

Dave shook his head. 'Now that poor Arthur is dead, it'll probably take the police longer to resolve things.'

Ellie cleared her throat. 'Um...' She blushed. 'Sylvia, Dave; in the spirit of full transparency, there's something I haven't told either of you yet.'

They both stared at her.

'Two things, actually. Firstly, Hayley is staying at Mary's. She's been there for a few days.'

'Hayley?' said Dave.

'Yup.' She brought them up to date. The dog dying, the camper van conking out. 'Something is going on with her. When the subject of Lloyd came up, she dashed out of the room and when I went to talk to her about him, she burst into tears.'

'How strange,' said Dave.

'I got the impression she hasn't said anything to Mary about Lloyd or why she's come back. You know what

Mary's like – very vague about things, and *laissez faire*. Doesn't ask questions.'

'Sounds like bliss,' muttered Dave.

'The second thing she told me is the biggie.'

'Oh? Now who's been concealing things?'

'I know. I agreed to keep quiet so she could tell you herself, but she's bottled. So, I said I'd fill you in. It's undoubtedly affecting her emotions and behaviour, *and* might be relevant to Lloyd's death, I don't know.'

'Come on,' said Sylvia. 'What is it?'

Ellie told them about the pregnancy.

'And she found out after the fight I had with Lloyd?' Dave looked at his mum. 'Crikey. What happened? Did she have the baby?'

'I don't know all the details. You'll have to ask her.'

Sylvia spoke slowly. 'How come we didn't know?'

Chapter 28

Ellie, Sylvia and Zoe were at the windmill kitchen table, about to start their team meeting. Dave had joined them.

'I'm so glad you're home, Gran.' Zoe was checking her phone for news of Sophie. 'We've run out of that millionaire's shortbread you made, and Finn is having withdrawal symptoms.' She kept her face straight for a few moments, then smiled. 'Joking.'

'Still nothing?' asked Ellie.

They were all worried about Sophie.

Zoe shook her head. 'D'you think she's going to be OK?'

'Er... I don't know.' She didn't want to give Zoe an empty guarantee or be too pessimistic. 'I very much hope so.'

'I'll check WhatsApp again.'

Dave stuffed the last bit of a sandwich into his mouth and brushed crumbs off his hands.

'I'd forgotten how much more food gets eaten when you're here,' said Ellie.

'Then there's the spooning stuff into his mouth when he's at the fridge,' said Zoe. 'He thinks we don't see him.'

'Oh, hello, Little Miss Hypocrite.' He chuckled. 'I've seen you doing that. And make me feel guilty, why don't you? I can go home. It's just, without work, it's... well... weird there on my own.'

'You need some hobbies, Dad.' Zoe plonked a kitten on his lap.

The lunchtime news was on the TV in the lounge as it was the only way they had of keeping up with developments in the police investigation.

'Now on BBC South East, the Canterbury lorry driver who killed a man last week has been charged with death by reckless driving.'

Ellie's ears pricked up. 'This is the man you mentioned,' she said to Dave, and rushed into the other room to hear better, the others following her.

'We are going live to Lower Wootton and local GP and founder of the SLOW IT DOWN campaign, Dr Peters. Dr Peters was a prominent voice a few years ago when local man, Lloyd Durden, ran down and killed lollipop lady, Joan Chapman, on a pedestrian crossing. Lloyd Durden was found dead at the weekend. Let's get his reaction now. Dr Peters, what can you tell us about this latest death?'

The camera showed the doctor standing on the pavement by the crossing where Joan was killed. As the presenter spoke, the traffic roared past. Buses, lorries, cars and vans, bicycles.

'Morning, Emily. Well, we are of course very sad to hear of another needless death on our roads and our hearts go out to all those involved. We welcome the opportunity here at SLOW IT DOWN to get a robust debate going on driving behaviour and speed. As long as these selfish drivers are at large on our roads, no-one is safe. As you can see from the traffic here, some vehicles are driving responsibly, others aren't.'

'He's so right,' said Sylvia. 'We really need to do something before someone else gets killed. Signs, humps in the road. Anything.'

'Just over two years ago, as you mentioned, we had the tragic death of our beloved lollipop lady – who was one of my patients. On this very crossing.'

Dr Peters was shaking his head in obvious sadness.

'Since then, there have been thousands more deaths in the UK due to drivers racing through villages and ignoring speed limits. You may remember that Lloyd Durden, prior to killing Joan, had been campaigning to have the speed limits increased on the section of the road where he killed Joan, and pushing to have the pedestrian crossing removed.'

'I still can't believe he was doing this,' Dave muttered. 'And, after killing poor Joan, and going to prison for it, he expected to come back and live here in the village happily ever after.'

'We've also got Damian South with us,' said the presenter.

'Oh, I was on a committee with him,' said Sylvia. 'The absolute gall of the man. I can't stand him.'

'Mr South runs an award-winning podcast called TIMES HAVE CHANGED,' said the presenter.

'Award-winning?' Sylvia sneered. 'He must've got his buddies to vote for him.'

The presenter continued, *'Mr South, what's your view on the objections that organisations such as SLOW IT DOWN are talking about?'*

'I think it's woke nonsense. People need to accept the fact we aren't living in tiny villages with cobbled streets and horse-drawn carts anymore. We all lead busy lives and drive vehicles. Research shows that slowing traffic down increases pollution, petrol consumption and vehicle noise, and does not reduce accidents.'

Ellie groaned. So, this was where Lloyd had got his 'facts' from. 'Sadly, some of that is true.'

'What happened to Mrs Chapman was tragic. But Lloyd was one of our members. We fully supported his efforts in Lower Wootton.'

'Dr Peters, what do you say to that?'

'I say that Mr South is the one who's out of touch. He's the perfect example of a rich townie, who takes up life in the country – and then wants to change it and make everyone else dance to his tune. There's a lot of anger in our rural communities towards these thugs who act with apparent impunity.'

'Good for him.' Zoe grinned. 'Fight, fight.'

'Are you calling me a thug?' Damian snarled into his webcam.

'If the cap fits, wear it,' Dr Peters replied. *'But I'm referring to the drivers who, through their selfishness and recklessness, have killed others. Questions are being asked about why Lloyd Durden was released from prison on licence when there are delays in recalling offenders who don't comply. We caught Durden driving and reported him. Nothing happened.'*

'That's dreadful,' said Zoe. 'Was he given an automatic driving ban?'

'Yes,' said Dave. 'As part of his sentence.'

Dr Peters continued. *'I wouldn't mind betting that the family of the man who was killed last week by the lorry driver are asking similar questions too. What I'd like to ask Mr South is, how would he feel if his mother or his wife or his daughter were mowed down by a driver?'*

'Would you like to come back on that, Mr South?' asked the presenter.

'Yes. I would want to know what they were doing in the middle of the road when vehicles were on it. It's as simple as that. You don't have train speeds reduced when they go

through villages, or people dawdling along on the rail tracks. Why should cars be made to slow down?'

'Back to you, Dr Peters. I believe you have a new campaign at SLOW IT DOWN. Is that right?'

'Yes, Emily. We're calling on Parliament through our local MP to increase the sentence given for this sort of selfish crime, and to disallow perpetrators from pleading guilty in order to reduce their sentence. We are also calling for stricter controls of licence breaches so convicts can't simply jump back behind the wheel when they're released and knock someone else down.'

'Viewers will remember,' said the presenter, *'Lloyd Durden pleaded guilty and had his sentence reduced by a third. He was also released early, as is policy.'*

'Exactly,' Dr Peters replied, *'and he told officials he was full of remorse. Yet, despite his ban, we saw him driving.'*

The news topic changed and the four of them returned to the kitchen table for their meeting.

Ellie took the lid off her pen. 'OK, we've got a lot to discuss so I suggest we adopt our usual procedure and review suspects, motives and key developments, and decide on our next steps.'

'Wow,' said Dave. 'So, this is how amateur sleuthing works? I'm impressed. You need to join the police.'

'Dad, that's a bit condescending.'

'Not really.' He looked shocked. 'Just an observation.'

Ellie ignored them, saying simply to Dave, 'You'll need to pick things up as we go along but most of it you should know about.'

'Shall I start?' asked Zoe.

'Go for it, lovey.'

'OK, so, basically, since Lloyd was killed there's been another death, and we have no idea who killed either of them.' She stuck out her bottom lip. 'And Dad might still go to prison.'

The three of them stared at her.

Ellie was aware Zoe was struggling with knowing her father had been arrested.

'That's not going to happen,' said Dave.

'And it's not as bad as that,' Ellie replied, keen to counter Zoe's negativity without putting her down. 'We know it's very likely that the same person killed both people.'

'We have circumstantial evidence against a number of people but nothing concrete,' added Sylvia. 'And that applies to motives as well.'

'Let's start by considering who our suspects are for Lloyd's murder,' said Ellie. 'Zo, what d'you reckon?'

Zoe took a deep breath. 'People who had grievances against Lloyd. His sister, Lydia. Amy's aunt, Belinda. Dr Peters. Joan's son, Ian.' She paused, glancing at Dave. 'We need to include you, Dad, as we don't know what the police's current thinking is.'

Dave grunted.

'She's right,' Sylvia chimed in support of Zoe. 'We do.'

'Any other suspects?' asked Dave. 'What about people who weren't part of Joan's death? And – I've got to ask. Do we think Hayley's pregnancy might have anything to do with Lloyd's death?'

Silence.

Sylvia was the first to speak. 'Until we've talked to her, and got the full picture, I don't see how we can know. I've arranged for us to meet her in the pub tomorrow morning.'

'Who else?' asked Ellie.

'The problem is,' said Sylvia, 'there are likely to be people we don't know about. For example, people Lloyd met in prison. But we can't name them because we don't know who they are. All we can do is flag them up as a potential suspect group.'

'It would be good to find out a bit more about Lloyd's time inside,' said Dave. 'I can't approach the prison governor without getting into trouble.'

'Ah,' Sylvia said. 'Now, I made a call about this. One of my old social work colleagues, Ralph, was going to see if he could find out whether there were any people Lloyd had conflict with while he was in prison, and who might have wanted to cause him harm.'

'That would be handy to know,' said Dave.

'I'll chase him up when we've finished. I wouldn't mind betting that Lloyd ticked people off in there. He can't help himself.'

'What about Arthur's death?' asked Dave. 'Should we be considering the same suspects?'

'When we know who they are, yes,' Sylvia replied, 'but we don't know enough yet to say, do we?'

Ellie turned back a page in her pad. 'The questions I have about Arthur are: was he killed because he knew who murdered Lloyd? Was he killed because of the support he showed to his son before and after prison?'

'Those are key, aren't they?' said Dave. 'Especially since he told you he knew who killed Lloyd.'

'Given we know much less about Arthur's death,' said Sylvia, 'let's go back to Lloyd's. Start there.'

'I agree,' said Ellie. 'One of the things we've rather overlooked is people's alibis. Ian told us he and his wife walked the dog together in Appledown Woods on Saturday morning. The problem is the pathologist estimated Lloyd's time of death at between 3am and 5am.'

'Which means Ian's alibi doesn't count as they walked later than that,' said Zoe. 'We'll need to ask him again.'

'Lydia told me she was out on Saturday night at bridge, and came home around 9pm and went to bed. So, she doesn't have an alibi either. I would like to speak to her again. See what she's got to say about her father's death.' Sylvia paused. 'There was no love lost between her and Lloyd, but she might be a bit more forthcoming given her dad is sadly now dead too.'

'We haven't talked to Dr Peters yet or Amy's aunt, Belinda,' said Ellie. 'They're due this afternoon. We'll have more to reflect on this evening.'

'Right,' said Sylvia. 'What noteworthy developments do we need to discuss?'

'Is Dad still a person of interest to the police?' Zoe came straight out with it.

Ellie turned to Dave. 'What have they said to you?'

'Very little. The chief superintendent still wants me on gardening leave. The chief inspector has requested I stay in the village in case they need me for further questioning.'

Sylvia tutted.

'I've no way of finding out about police developments without seriously jeopardising my future. I'm *still* not allowed to access my work email in case I'm accidentally copied in on material that's sensitive to the investigation.'

'That's understandable. Don't worry. I'm sure they'll reinstate you very soon. It's not as if you've been in any trouble before, have you?'

Dave looked down.

'Dad?'

'Have you?' Ellie repeated.

Dave closed his eyes as though his worst nightmare had just come true. He shook his head regretfully.

'Wait,' said Ellie, trying not to screech. 'Please don't tell me there's something else you haven't told me about?'

'Nope. I was just kidding.' He glanced at Ellie and Zoe. 'Seriously though – how quick were you guys to think the worst of me?'

Chapter 29

'I called at the surgery and Lydia said you've got the afternoon off,' Ellie told Dr Peters. 'I hope you don't mind me coming round to the house.'

'Ellie.' The GP straightened up and smiled. 'No, not at all.'

He was in the back garden, on the patio, standing in front of a pile of logs, an axe in his hand. He'd paired a brown casual jacket with his work trousers.

'We caught your interview on BBC South East earlier. About the SLOW IT DOWN campaign.'

He groaned. 'Was I frightfully bad-tempered? I've been on programmes with Damian before and he incenses me. He's a city banker who's taken up country life.' He swung the axe, bringing it down on a large lump of oak.

'I don't blame you for one moment. We were watching on the TV and were all ready to scream at him. Sylvia can't stand him either.'

'Anyway – to what do I owe the honour? You don't generally pop round. Are you three investigating Lloyd and Arthur's murders?'

'Yes. This wasn't one I wanted to get involved with at all but, as always, someone seems to need our help.'

'Ah. The newspaper article. Dave.' He laid the axe down. 'Shall we perch for a moment?' He steered her towards their garden furniture.

On the table, a mug of tea was untouched.

'Yes. I was wondering if you bumped into Lloyd before he died.' She lowered herself onto a wooden bench. 'So far, I've spoken to two people who were desperately hoping to avoid him and didn't manage it.'

To their left, a large lawn stretched down to a pond and wooden bridge.

'I bet half the village had been hoping to avoid him.' He sat on a chair facing Ellie. 'I don't know why he couldn't have gone to live somewhere else. But, to answer your question, I did have the misfortune of running into him.

I suppose in a small village like ours it's not easy to avoid someone.'

'Where was this?'

'Doing the day job. He booked a GP appointment with me. Unfortunately, I'm his doctor. Wish I'd removed him from the practice register while he was in prison, although I don't know if that would have been ethical. It certainly would have averted our encounter.'

'How'd it go?' Ellie was wondering whether it was a legitimate medical consultation or some sort of ruse to gain access to Dr Peters.

'He had a number of medical issues which hadn't been managed adequately when he was in prison. Booked a double appointment, which I appreciated, but unfortunately at the end he started on about the speed campaign and how he was still right about reduced speeds not decreasing accident numbers.'

'Oh dear.'

'Quite.'

A black cat crept into view in front of a hydrangea. It made a beeline for Ellie and jumped up on her lap, purring loudly. 'Hello,' she said stroking it.

'That's Jemima.'

Ellie told him about the kittens and then mentioned Lloyd. 'Why did he think that was an appropriate time and place to raise the issue?'

'I've no idea. I suspect he simply just couldn't stop himself. Maybe he couldn't resist the chance to wind me up. Who knows? Lloyd was a man of impulse not reason, although he liked to pretend otherwise.'

'Did he get aggressive?' Ellie was thinking about Lloyd's visit to Dave.

'I would say passive-aggressive rather than aggressive.' He took a pack of mints out of his pocket, popped one in his mouth and passed them to Ellie.

'No, thanks.'

'At the end of the appointment, he lingered and tried to use his body weight and size to intimidate me, sort of leaning over my desk and staring me out. Walking slowly across the room, even though I said I needed to get on and see my next patient.'

'Did he discuss his mental health at all? Mention any concerns he had?'

'I'm mindful of patient confidentiality so can't disclose what we discussed. However, I assume what you mean is, did he mention anything that might help with understanding his murder?'

'Yes, exactly.'

'He was convinced someone was following him and seemed extremely anxious about it.'

'I'll leave the anxiety part. Did you give him any advice about thinking he was being followed?'

Jemima jumped off Ellie's lap and sauntered over to her owner, brushing against his legs.

'I told him to go to the police. I'm afraid I wasn't particularly sympathetic. With hindsight, it would have been better for one of the other doctors to have seen him. I found it difficult to treat him objectively. I was the first person on the scene when he ran Joan down and, to this day, I haven't been able to get that image out of my head.'

'I'm sure no one would blame you for that.'

'I didn't realise he'd booked an appointment with me. Unless we actively look to see who is on our list, whoever walks into our room is a surprise. So, I only found out that I was seeing him when he shuffled in.' He shrugged. 'I suppose at that point I could have refused to see him and got him transferred to a colleague, but he quickly sat down and launched into his medical concerns. So, I just thought I might as well get on with it and see him out.' He shook his head slightly, his eyes closed, as though he was embarrassed about what he was describing. 'I don't feel great about that, particularly given what's happened.' He gestured to the logs. 'Fortunately, this is rather cathartic.'

'It sounds like you dealt with his medical concerns professionally and thoroughly. He got the double appointment he booked. And you suggested he take his other concerns to the police. I don't think there's anything for you to feel bad about particularly. As you say, hindsight is a wonderful thing.' She paused. 'Do you know if he went to the police?'

Dr Peters shook his head. 'Unfortunately, I don't know. I had him escorted out of my room in the end because he kept delaying leaving. And a few days later, he was dead.'

'Have you told the police Lloyd thought someone was following him or watching him? Apparently, he said the same to Amy.'

'Yes. I did tell them. And about the medical consultation.'

'Did the police ask you where you were early Saturday morning?'

'The alibi question. Yes. My wife and I had friends round for dinner. Finished around 11pm and we went to bed about half an hour later, after clearing up. We then got up about 8.30am on Saturday. It wasn't early, anyway. Neither of us had work. My wife left the house just before ten for a hair appointment at Helen's in the high street.'

'Thank you. And if you had to guess who killed him, what would you say?'

He sucked air in through his mouth. 'Now you're asking.' He met her gaze, eyes blinking. 'We all know how many people disliked him. How many people he'd rubbed up the wrong way with his stupid speed campaign. How many people were incensed over his reckless driving and Joan's tragic death. But they're all friends and family members of ours.'

Ellie knew exactly what he meant.

'Putting aside for one moment how angry we all are about what he did, would any of them – any of *us* – actually want him dead?' He kept his gaze on Ellie. 'There's a big difference between wishing someone was dead, even fantasising about it, and actually doing something to bring it about.'

'I know,' Ellie replied. 'I've been having the same problem. I always feel privileged to help people when we're conducting investigations, but my goodness, it's not easy investigating family and friends.'

'And while it's easy to think his murder is related to Joan's death, the truth is he'd been in prison for two years. It's perfectly possible he got mixed up with something unsavoury while he was inside.'

That was true.

'Or – you know how he liked to wind people up – maybe he chose the wrong person this time?'

Chapter 30

Sylvia dusted the pastry with flour and rolled it. The apple filling was ready. Touch of clove and cinnamon. Just the way she liked it.

Outside, Sarge had arrived. He was standing, as was customary, with his hands on his hips surveying the garden as if it was one of the areas of the nursery where he still worked. In his layers of clothing, all a different shade of khaki, it wasn't immediately obvious how frail he was, but Sylvia knew. He'd reduced his work hours further – much to their disappointment – and that meant more time for him to spend in Ellie's large garden at the windmill, where he could choose his pace.

As Sylvia watched, Rebus scuttled about following scents and chasing Finn's cat, Mouse, who'd taken to skulking outside while Tabitha and the kittens were in residence. Rebus seemed to sense that Sarge was physically vulnerable. He would slow down as he approached the old man, rather than ramming into him, as he did with everyone else. When he jumped up, he did it gently, often resting a pleading paw on Sarge's arm.

This afternoon, Dave was outside too, seemingly still not wanting to return home to his flat while he was on leave. The two men had met numerous times before, but this was the first time they'd both been in Ellie's garden together on their own. And Sylvia was captivated by the dynamics.

She stretched the pastry over the tray, dolloped the sweet-smelling apple filling into the cups, and cut round each one. As she worked, she watched and listened. And through the open window, she heard their conversation.

A movement caught her attention.

One of the kittens jumped from the ground up onto the garden furniture.

She banged on the window, and yelled, 'Quick. A kitten's out. On the chair.'

Dave turned round. He geared up for what looked like a lunge and seemed to change his mind. Crept up on the unsuspecting kitten instead and swooped it up. 'Just one out here, I think. I'll have a good look round. D'you want to take this one?' He passed the furry creature to his mum through the window, then searched where they'd been standing. 'All clear, I think.'

Francesca would be home in the morning. Sylvia knew Ellie would be relieved to get back to her bed, but they'd miss the kittens.

Dave returned to Sarge.

'The floribunda needs pruning, right enough,' said Sarge.

Sylvia was used to his pronouncements. You were never sure whether he was talking to himself or you, but she rather liked it regardless.

'Improves its health and lifespan, so it does,' Sarge continued in his usual half-sentences. 'Encourages growth too. Clean cuts with sharp secateurs. Can use loppers or a pruning saw on the larger stems.'

This time it sounded like he was talking to Dave.

Dave, in turn, stared at him. Sylvia saw him slip his phone out of his pocket then change his mind. 'The flori-what?'

'Rose. Large one over there.' He pointed at the wall. 'A couple of the stems are diseased, I noticed. Need cutting right back, they do.'

'Gotcha. Want a hand?'

'Know how to use loppers, do you?'

'Er...'

'Take your pick. There's the rose. The perennial clumps need dividing.' He pointed to a flowerbed by the outhouse. 'Weeds to hoe in all the beds. And summer flowering bulbs to get in.'

Dave's neck was on a swivel as he tried to pinpoint the things Sarge was referring to.

'We don't use slug pellets because of the dog.'

'Course. Yeah. Thanks.'

'We're having potatoes this year for the first time. Need to get the early ones in.'

'Right. Well, point me in the right direction, give me the right tool and tell me what to do.' His smile reminded Sylvia of Dave as a young boy, eager to learn from his dad, appreciative of the companionship and the opportunity to engage in a simple task he knew nothing about.

Bet Dave was pleased Sarge didn't ask nosey questions. Sarge might be Mary's age, but he knew what was going on. Just pretended he didn't.

'Let's fetch you a spade. Get you digging the bed for the potatoes. That's probably the easiest, right enough. You'll need some better footwear though. Can't dig properly in trainers. You'll get mud all over them. Come with me.' He marched Dave off to the outhouse.

Half an hour later, they were still at it, so Sylvia took them out mugs of tea and a chocolate brownie each.

'My lad and I have been planting the summer flowering bulbs in the graveyard,' Sarge told them. 'The vicar, he liked the gladioli we put in last year, he did. Think we'll add some agapanthus this year.'

Sarge's 'lad' was his great-nephew, Sean.

'How's Sean's gardening business going?' asked Sylvia.

'Taken off like a rocket, it has. He'll be doing the church on his own soon. Getting too much for me. There's only so far I can keep pushing my back. I've avoided being in a wheelchair for fifty years. Don't want to end up in one now.'

'I'm sure you'll still be on hand to give him advice when he needs it.'

Sarge spluttered. 'He doesn't need any advice from me these days. Knows more than I do. And all the new fancy systems. Anyway, these days, at the graveyard, it's mostly cutting the grass and picking up beer cans and litter. And shooing the snoggers off the benches.' He tutted and put on a shocked face.

'Are there more snoggers than usual then?' asked Dave through a grin.

Sylvia pictured lustful teenagers, grabbing illicit moments away from prying parents.

'Either that or they don't have any other places to meet. There's one couple who come in, regular as clockwork.' He rolled his eyes exaggeratedly. 'It's as if they can't wait to be together. And all that talking in baby language to each other.' He snorted. 'I wish they'd take their rubbish home with them, rather than leave it for others to pick up. Last time the girl dropped a red lipstick. Keep meaning to get Sean to put a post on the Wootton Facebook page in case the owner wants it bac–'

Sylvia interrupted him. 'What was the lipstick like?'

'No point asking me that. Soil, plants, fertiliser, yes. Women's make-up. No chance. It's in my jacket pocket though, if you want a look-see.' He pointed to a padded jacket that was hanging on the back of a garden fork.

Sylvia scuttled over, slid the jacket off and brought it over.

Arthur retrieved the lipstick and handed it to her. It wasn't a make she recognised, but she knew who would know where it was from.

Zoe.

'I'll get Finn or Zoe to put a post on Facebook,' Sylvia told him. 'Don't worry.'

Dave laughed. 'Ah, young love. Don't you remember?' he said to Sarge mischievously. 'Eating sweets and snogging.'

The older man's face constricted. 'Can't say I do, no.'

Was he thinking back to his days in the circus? After his accident, and back injury, it had been as though parts of his life had come – quite literally – to a crashing halt.

Sylvia wondered how Sarge felt about it, and if his life would be like that forever.

Chapter 31

'It was priceless.' Sylvia was telling Ellie about Sarge and Dave in the garden. 'But very sweet.'

They were on their way to see Amy's aunt, via the village hardware shop in the high street.

'I wonder whose the lipstick is that Sarge found,' said Ellie. 'I don't know many people who wear that deep red. Sophie does, Fran's daughter. She's an artist and it suits her long black hair.'

They'd arrived at the shop. It was a treasure trove of a place, which had been run by a husband-and-wife team for the last fifteen years. Brooms of all sizes stood in racks outside. The key cutting machine was always busy and Neil Thompson prided himself in getting people's keys right first time.

The doorbell dinged as they entered. It was a large space, rammed with tall shelves, laden with products.

Sylvia's eyes fell on a long handle dustpan and brush. Would be handy for all the crumbs Dave dropped, walking round the house eating toast.

While Ellie hunted for picture wire, she approached the man behind the counter and introduced herself. She told him about Blix Investigators. 'A rather strange question, I'm afraid. Have you sold any picture wire recently?'

'*I* haven't. Let me check the book. My wife might have.' He leafed through the notepad by the till. 'No. None in March. It's not very popular these days.' They chatted about the pros and cons of hooks versus wire. 'You know the thing I get asked for most at the moment? Fishing bait.'

'What's that about then?' asked Sylvia. 'I mean, why the rush on bait all of a sudden?'

'Couldn't tell you. Some chap's been in several times. Never seen him until a week or so ago. And one of the people who bought a lot,' he lowered his voice to a whisper, *'was Lloyd Durden.'*

Chapter 32

'Thanks for talking to us,' Ellie told Belinda.

'Amy told us you were strongly opposed to her marrying Lloyd,' said Sylvia. 'Could you tell us a bit about that?'

'Sure,' Belinda replied.

They were in her lounge, a room so small, a two-seater sofa only just fitted along the longest wall.

Belinda gestured to the sofa and made her way to an armchair by the fireplace, tucking a pen into the breast pocket of her dark blue uniform.

Sylvia sat down.

On the mantelpiece, next to a vase of daffodils, a collection of photographs caught Ellie's attention. In one, Amy and her aunt were sitting next to each other on a hay bale in the sun, both with sunglasses perched on the top of their head, drinking ginger beer and giggling.

'She's always been pretty,' said Ellie, picking it up for a closer look.

'The summer fair, that was.' Sadness leaked into Belinda's voice. 'Before Lloyd was released.' Her expression was wistful. 'I doubt much of what I'm going to tell you will come as a shock, given you both live in the village and have been looking into this case for a few days.'

Ellie put the photo back and settled herself next to Sylvia. The room was uncluttered and cosy.

'Something I realised as a social worker,' said Sylvia, 'is it's easy to think we know everything about a person, but the truth is we very rarely do. Even those we live with and are closest to. Everyone has secrets, don't they?'

Her words were poignant, and Ellie wondered how her mother-in-law viewed the subject given what she now knew about her husband and son.

Belinda nodded. 'Yes. There have certainly been things which Amy didn't know about Lloyd, which I found out.'

Ellie and Sylvia exchanged glances.

'I've known for a long time they wanted to get married. I mean, they'd been a couple for donkeys' years. Of course, I hoped they would go off the idea or the relationship would fizzle out.'

She wrinkled her nose, as though it made her feel guilty to say aloud what she'd probably kept to herself for years.

'To be honest, I was staggered it survived Joan's death and him going to prison.' She glanced at them, and Ellie got the impression she was checking to see how her words were landing. 'I hoped Amy would see sense and dump him, but she didn't. If anything, she seemed to double down on her loyalty and was even more determined that they'd get married.'

She rolled her eyes, her frustration evident. 'Amy's mother, my sister, didn't share my view. She was much more forgiving of Lloyd than I ever have been, and was of the opinion it was up to Amy to decide for herself who she wanted to marry.'

'It must have been very difficult for all of you,' said Ellie, not wanting to disturb Belinda's flow.

'The thing is, I've known about something that happened a long time ago that isn't – shall we say – common knowledge.'

Sylvia sat up. 'Oh?'

Belinda continued. 'Lloyd was never able to get his wandering eye in check. When he was in his late teens, he cheated on a young girlfriend and broke her heart.'

Sylvia nodded sadly. 'Are you talking about my daughter?'

'You know?' Belinda let out a sigh of relief and placed her hand on her chest.

'Only as of this morning. Hayley told Ellie yesterday. Dave didn't know either.'

'In that case, I don't want to...' She broke off.

'No, please tell us whatever you know. It all helps us to understand.'

'Predictably, he behaved abominably. Having got her pregnant, he then abandoned her.'

'Man's a complete rat,' said Sylvia. 'It's a good job he's de–'

Ellie nudged her.

'Probably got freaked out about the idea of impending fatherhood and the inevitable restrictions to his lifestyle,' said Belinda. 'Left her high and dry and continued running round with Amy.'

'Did Amy know Hayley had got pregnant?' asked Sylvia.

'I don't think so. I didn't tell her until much later as it wasn't my place to divulge something as delicate as that.'

'How did *you* know about all of this?' asked Ellie, glancing at Sylvia, who was sitting very still.

'I'm a nurse.' She gestured to her uniform. 'I've been one since I left school. I was working at the doctor's practice when Hayley came in with Ron. They were both absolutely devastated.' Belinda's voice was a whisper. 'Look, I don't want to cause trouble. I've seen what happens with secrets like this.' She chewed her lip. 'I can tell you what I know. The truth is, I'm not sure how much is relevant to Lloyd's death.'

Ellie's brain was working at a hundred miles an hour.

'I'll let you know about something else. I had a private investigator tracking Lloyd's activities ever since he came out of prison.'

'Ah,' said Ellie. 'Was this a man or a woman?'

'Man, why? And I say "private investigator" but...'

Ellie explained. 'Amy said Lloyd thought he was being followed, and had the impression it was by a woman.'

'Lloyd was drunk most of the time. He probably didn't even notice, let alone see whether it was a man or woman.' Belinda gave a regretful sigh.

'You mean he made up that he was being followed?' asked Sylvia.

'Perfectly possible,' Belinda replied. 'For attention or sympathy. To get other people into trouble. Who knows?' She rolled her eyes. 'I gave up years ago asking him to be honest with Amy and me. The man was pathologically incapable of telling the truth. That's why I decided to take matters into my own hands. Especially when she said they'd decided to tie the knot.'

'Did Amy know about the PI?'

'Yes. It was a radical enough action to take on my part and it didn't feel ethical to do it without not just Amy's knowledge but her consent. As it turned out, she didn't mind at all and even suggested someone she knew who'd done personal protection and security.'

'So, when *did* Amy find out about the pregnancy?'

'I'm not absolutely sure. I think – this is what she's told me – the first she learned of it was when I told her around five years ago. But there has always been some collusion on Amy's part where Lloyd is concerned. So, whether she knew before that and chose to turn a blind eye, I don't know.'

Ellie was trying to decide if this could be related to Lloyd's death. It was impossible to know at the moment. Hopefully, Hayley would level with them when they met her. Say what happened and why she'd come back to the village.

'I'm really sorry you're hearing some of this from me.' Belinda's gaze was on Sylvia, who was now by the window. 'It wasn't my place at the time to say anything. As a practice nurse, I was bound by patient confidentiality and, even if I hadn't been, it still wouldn't have felt right to start asking people what they did and didn't know. I left that up to your husband and Arthur Durden.' She leaned over in her seat in an effort to catch Sylvia's eye. 'All I can tell you is they were very concerned about your daughter's welfare.'

Chapter 33

Sylvia shot out of Belinda's. 'How could Ron take Hayley to the doctor without telling me?' She muttered under her breath over and over. 'She was pregnant, for goodness' sake.'

Ellie offered company but Sylvia was adamant she wanted to be alone.

Ellie got into the jeep thinking about people who could have seen something relevant to either of the murders. The news of Hayley's pregnancy had dragged them all into an emotional quagmire, and Ellie was determined to pull them out of it.

They were badly lacking eye-witnesses. The police would be doing house-to-house calls around the Durden family home, so it was best not to interfere there for now.

She rang Zoe.

'Mum?'

'I want to find out whether the people who live in the cottage on the lane that leads into the hare meadow saw or heard anything. You said you noticed the owner opening the curtains when you walked past. That would have been quite early. I'm pretty sure the lady who lives there is elderly.'

'She is,' said Zoe. 'But I was there after Lloyd was killed, don't forget.'

'That's true. She might have been up earlier though. If she has insomnia, people often get up and nip to the loo or fetch themselves a drink.'

'I know her a little. She lives there with her disabled husband. When I'm walking Rebus, I often see them. The husband likes to sit at the window in his wheelchair, soaking up the sun and looking out.'

'If they were up in the early hours, it's worth asking what they remember. She might have heard screaming, for example.'

'Why don't we go now? Come and pick me up and I'll come with you.'

When Ellie arrived back at the windmill to collect Zoe, the news was blaring out on the TV, and no-one was in sight. Ellie couldn't wait for the investigation to be over, so they could switch off the TV and get a bit of peace.

'Hello-o?' She shouted over the noise.

'Up here, Mum,' Zoe shouted back. 'The kittens have learnt how to climb the staircase.'

'Bet it's the small one with the fierce markings. The one that got into the jeep.'

'Yep. She's the ringleader alright. I've called her Tallulah. Anyway, I've got three of them. Be down in a sec.'

Ellie filled the pets' water bowls and said hello to Tabitha, who was curled up on the soil of Ellie's weeping fig.

Zoe carried the three kittens into the office. 'We need a cat babygate,' she said over her shoulder to her mum. 'A catgate,' she joked. 'Perhaps Dad can knock one up.'

'We're bringing you some breaking news now,' said the TV presenter.

'Right. What's this going to be?' asked Ellie.

'Brendan Murphy, who is wanted by police for breaking the terms of his probation, has been sighted in a number of locations in Kent.'

'Mum. Come and listen to this.'

'He has family in Margate. Members of the public saw him at McDonald's in Dover. A bus driver saw him boarding one of their vehicles in the Deal area of Kent, heading towards the village of Lower Wootton.'

'So, he's come over this way.'

'Mr Murphy has a number of tattoos, which might help with identification. In particular, a raven on the top of his head.'

An image flashed up on the TV of a shaven-headed man, with black ink over his skull.

'Wow.'

'Police are advising the public not to approach Mr Murphy, and to call 999 with any information.'

'Let's get out of here,' said Ellie. 'Make sure the office door is shut, lovey, can you? We won't be long. We can leave Tabitha in the lounge. Fran said that's fine for an hour or so.'

The white house near the hare meadow was a double-fronted, rendered building, set back from the footpath. It had a powder-blue door, and matching blue frames around wooden sash windows. On the first floor, shutters hung either side of each window, all in the same blue. Above the front door sat a large porthole window.

The old lady said their name was Gardner. 'Marjorie and Norman Gardner. Would you like to come in?'

'Thanks,' said Zoe. 'I brought my mum with me. We're private investigators and we're looking into the murder of the man who was found in the pond in the hare meadow.' She paused, seemingly realising she was gabbling. 'We were wondering whether you saw or heard anything in the early hours of Saturday morning?'

'The police asked us this. Something spooked our dog just after 4am. Set him off, barking and barking until I came down. I didn't know at first if it was the foxes, or the wind in the barn making something bang, but it must have been the people walking by.'

'What people?'

'Walking past. I know what time it was because our grandfather clock was striking as I was coming downstairs.'

'And who was it?'

'A couple of people, carrying fishing equipment. Nothing fancy, like. Just rods, a net and a shopping bag. Bait, probably.'

'Was one of them Lloyd?' Zoe showed the woman a mugshot of Lloyd from the police website.

'I don't know, dear. I wasn't close enough to see. Looked like they were two men though.'

Chapter 34

Later that evening, Zoe, Finn and Ellie were in the office, replaying the videos that Zoe had taken of the hare meadow and pond on the morning of Lloyd's death. They wanted to see if there were any people about, or clues that might advance the investigation. Zoe's camera was linked up to the desktop so they could see them on the large monitor.

'Look at the hares,' said Finn. 'Aren't they striking? The light makes their golden-brown fur seem almost red.'

'And the grass looks semi-translucent,' Zoe replied. 'Gran and I went to a talk at Deal Castle on British wildlife. It's what gave me the idea for the competition. These are brown hares. They were introduced into the UK in the Iron Age.'

'Get you. Ms Wildlife Expert,' teased Finn affectionately.

'It's the mating season. They box like that because the males are being over-persistent in their desire for a mate.' She sighed. 'It goes on for weeks.'

'No wonder hares are revered as fertility symbols,' Finn replied.

On the film, the early morning rays beamed down through a slight haze onto dewy grass. A cuckoo sounded, high up in the poplars behind the pond.

Finn nudged her. 'You've definitely got to use one of these images for the competition. Look at the light on the water, under the willow branches.'

'Yes, it's beautiful. This was when I started following the hares across the meadow. See?' Zoe traced where her movements would have been, off screen. 'This is when I heard the ducks on the pond. I turned when I heard that coot come up for air.'

'There's Lloyd's body.' Finn increased the sound volume on the video. 'What's that noise? Like metal grinding against metal. And a gate clanging. I heard it earlier too, before you came into the field.' He stopped the video and rewound it. 'There it is. Weird. I wonder what it is.'

'They're building a new housing development two fields on from the hare meadow, near the station,' said Ellie. 'Could the workmen have been moving heavy equipment at night?'

'It's definitely that sort of sound, isn't it?' He frowned momentarily and pursed his lips in thought. 'Anyway. No matter. Let's see what surrounds that meadow. I know there's the lane where the white house is.'

'Why don't we check Google maps?' Ellie suggested. 'It's easy to forget places, or think they're further away – or nearer – than they are.'

'That's a good idea,' Finn replied. 'It's so true. I didn't know there was an old church tucked away in a side road on the way out of Lower Wootton. It's pretty much disused now. Stumbled on it the other morning when Charlie and I were running.'

Finn clicked on Google maps, entered the address and selected Street View. The meadow came into view, and the pond. The lane with the white house. St Mary's church. The high street. Appledown Woods. The station.

'I'll play the noise again,' he said. 'See what we think it is.'

He clicked on the video and they all watched and listened. They heard Zoe's breathing. Her feet on the flinty path. The cuckoo. Then the sound they'd heard and the clanging gate.

'I suppose the builders could have been working at night. I've seen them sometimes, with huge lights.' Ellie felt a welcome flicker of hope. 'If they were about, one of them might have seen something.'

'Could be the site,' said Zoe. 'Or – how close is the meadow to the railway line and Lower Wootton station?'

Finn went back to Google and switched to the map. 'As the crow flies, the station is about half a mile. But the line isn't far at all. Look, it goes along behind the hedges here.' He pointed at the dotted black line on the map.

'Actually,' Ellie remembered, 'Sally and I saw a flyer at Coldblow Crossing, saying Network South East were going to do engineering work at night. I can't remember what the dates were, but it'll be on the Lower Wootton Facebook page, I'm sure.' She looked at Finn. 'Could you play the clip again?'

They had another listen.

'That is definitely metal-on-metal,' said Ellie. 'You can hear the screeching.'

Zoe opened the browser on her phone and was quickly on the village Facebook page, scrolling through the recent posts. 'Here we are. Friday and Saturday nights, essential engineering works from 1200 to 0500.'

Ellie peered over her shoulder. 'That's what it is then. The contractors are Fleming Rail Engineering. And – as I was hoping – there's a number.'

The three of them locked eyes briefly.

'I wonder if any of them might have caught sight of Lloyd and whoever went into the hare meadow and killed him. Give them a ring, Zo. See what they say.'

Chapter 35
TUESDAY

The next morning, Sylvia was up early, keen to get to the housing development that was being built near where Lloyd was killed. Zoe had rung ahead and been told to report to the main entrance.

'Hurry up, lovey,' Sylvia yelled up the stairs to Zoe, who was on the phone to Finn.

'Won't be a minute,' Zoe shouted back.

There was a bit more muffled conversation and then Zoe leaned over the bannisters and yelled down. 'Sophie's turned up.' She ran down, beaming. 'Three of them had a dodgy curry and were ill. She stayed with the band she sang with Monday night.'

'Oh, thank goodness. But why didn't she let her friends know?'

'She was expecting to come home and didn't take her charger with her. Her phone died. Everyone there had Android and hers is an iPhone, so she couldn't borrow a charger.'

'That's why it was going to voicemail,' Sylvia confirmed. 'Is she going to inform the police?'

'Yep.'

'And her mum?'

'She's rung her.'

Half an hour later, the two women were getting close to the building site. Before they arrived, the noise hit them. Pneumatic drills. Intermittent beeping. Shouting. Banging. The air was thick with fumes.

'Ugh. What's that smell?' asked Zoe.

'Cement dust.' Sylvia pointed at four giant silos which towered over black, wooden hoardings. These were taller than either of them and stretched as far as the eye could see.

'This place is far larger than I anticipated,' said Zoe. 'They don't want people to see in, do they?'

At the gates, a workman was waiting for them. High visibility vest, baggy trousers with lots of pockets and hard boots. He looked Sylvia up and down and winked at Zoe. 'Alright darlin'.'

'We're here to see Jon Melville,' Zoe told him. 'I spoke to him on the phone. We're from Blix Investigators.'

Sylvia felt a swell of pride for Zoe, who was becoming more and more confident with each investigation.

'Follow me,' the man growled, and marched them round the periphery of the site to a Portakabin. He knocked on the door. 'Boss?'

'Bring them in, Sam,' came a familiar gravelly voice from within the mini-office. 'I'll take it from here.'

Sam just about managed to stand aside to allow Sylvia and Zoe to climb up the steps. Sitting behind a large wooden desk was Fraser Monroe, a belligerent property developer they'd encountered on a previous case.

'Well, well, well. Jon said you'd been in touch.'

Sylvia was – for once – at a loss for words.

'If it isn't Wootton's very own Multiple Marples. I knew our paths would cross again at some point. Remind me why I should help you with your busybody sleuthing?'

A rush of anger helped Sylvia find her voice. 'I'm sure you've seen the news,' she snapped. 'Because two people have been killed and the village isn't safe. Plus, we would like to help get justice for everyone affected.'

'How noble,' he sneered, smoothing his wavy hair. 'We're working on a thirty-two-million-pound contract here. I'm afraid my staff don't have time to contribute to silly little amateur sleuthing.' His thin lips drew into a smug, rather cruel smile, and he sat back in his luxurious chair, relishing the power he had over them. 'If you'd spoken to *me*, I'd have saved you the trouble of schlepping over here for nothing.'

'But Jon's already found the CCTV,' said Zoe, inching towards his desk. 'He was doing it when we were on the phone. It won't take a minute for him to show us, and it could make all the difference.'

Monroe's face clouded over. 'I wasn't aware my foreman worked for *you*, Miss Blix. I've said no, and that means no. Or don't you understand that word?'

Zoe muttered.

'Sam?' he barked. 'Escort these *ladies* off site, will you?'

Sam stuck his head into the cabin. 'Shall we go?' This time he held the door open, allowing them out. 'Follow me.' He led them round the back of the Portakabin, where there was a vehicle track to the entrance.

As soon as they were out of Monroe's earshot, Zoe gave Sylvia a look which clearly meant something and spun round to the workman. 'Sorr-ee.' She made her tone apologetic. 'We shouldn't have come. I realise that now.' She pointed at the entrance. 'We'll see ourselves out. Don't worry. You get back to work.' She turned to Sylvia. 'Come on, Gran.' She slipped her arm through her grandmother's and dragged her off. 'Keep walking,' she hissed at Sylvia.

When they reached the entrance, Zoe spun round. 'The coast is clear. This is only going to work if we're quick.' She fished out her mobile, scrolled and dialled a number. 'Jon? Hi, it's Zoe Blix here. Mr Monroe's asked if you could come and collect us. He's just gone into a meeting.' She told him where they were and rung off.

'Let's hope he's quick,' said Sylvia, half expecting Sam to reappear and have a go at them.

'I'm pretty sure that's Jon's cabin there. He said he was right by the entrance.'

'Makes sense. He's the foreman.'

'Yep,' said Zoe, 'dog bowl outside. He mentioned that.'

A minute later, a grey head appeared round the door of the cabin Zoe had pointed out. He waved them over.

'Quick,' she said. 'Before someone sees us.'

They ran over.

Zoe introduced Sylvia and herself and they clambered up the steps. This cabin was much larger with several desks. A radio was blasting out pop hits. On each desk there was a computer with a widescreen monitor.

Jon turned the radio down. He was a portly man with a friendly face. Blue cotton shirt tucked into work trousers. 'I had a quick look at our CCTV. Checked we still have it for the period of 2.30am to 5am on Saturday morning.' He ushered them in. 'The cops were asking for it too, but Monroe wasn't having any of it.'

'Public-spirited of him,' said Sylvia. For a brief moment, she thought he was going to say it had been deleted, but surely he wouldn't have called them over, if so?

'The eastern camera has a clear view over the lane into the hare meadow. It shows a couple of fellas entering the field.'

'Brilliant,' squealed Zoe. 'Thank you.'

At last – a tangible piece of evidence.

Jon gestured to another man. 'I've asked Lucas to help you. He's much better with technology than me. Dreadful hair but he knows his stuff.' He smiled at his younger colleague.

Lucas got to his feet. 'Ladies,' he said. It was then they saw how tall he was. He rearranged his waxed quiff and walked over to greet them. 'Come and have a seat.' He pulled two chairs over and gestured to Sylvia and Zoe.

Once they were settled, Lucas turned his attention to the computer and tapped a couple of keys on the keyboard, displaying a moving image.

Zoe was tracking his every move, grinning, clearly in her nerdy element.

The screen showed high-resolution images of the lane, a path, a field, taken from a height. A large brown dog shot into view, chasing a rabbit. Then it showed a man and a woman, walking side by side along a path.

'He said it was two *guys*.' Zoe glanced over at Jon, expressing Sylvia's exact thought.

Lucas chuckled. 'Probably didn't have his glasses on,' he said quietly.

'I heard that,' Jon replied. 'Apologies, ladies. I literally only had a glance. And, to be fair, you were rabbiting in my ear.'

Lucas carried on clicking, refining the image, going from one frame to another.

'So, that's Lloyd,' said Sylvia. 'Who's the woman? All I can see is the back of her head.'

'You can see her face in a moment. Hang on.'

'Could you zoom in a bit please? I... er... forgot to bring *my* glasses.'

Normally Zoe would crack a joke at her gran's expense. It was testament to her captivation that she let the opportunity pass.

Lucas increased the scale.

Sylvia gasped. 'That's Hayley. That's my *daughter*. What an earth was she doing with Lloyd?'

'Are you sure?' asked Zoe. She hadn't seen Hayley for a few years and wasn't familiar with her frame and gait.

'Yes. I'd know that walk anywhere.' She turned to Lucas. 'Can you check the time stamp, please?'

'Sure,' said Lucas, 'but it's within the period your granddaughter specified.' He clicked a few keys. 'Here we go. 03:01.'

Sylvia's eyes flashed with alarm. 'What was she doing in the field with him in the middle of the night?'

'Don't know – but hopefully we'll find out in a couple of hours,' Zoe replied.

She produced a USB stick from her pocket. 'Could we get a copy of that, please?'

Lucas took the device from Zoe and after another couple of key presses, returned the USB to Zoe.

'Thanks for your help, both of you,' said Zoe.

'No problem,' said Jon. 'Hope your relative isn't... er... in trouble.'

And a few minutes later, they were leaving the building site and on their way back home.

Fraser Monroe was going to be furious when he found out. But that was his lookout.

More importantly – Sylvia needed to call Ellie and Dave. See what they made of this development.

Chapter 36

Ellie had always liked Goose Meadow, the old mansion house where Dave had his flat. It was a vast, red brick building, with Gothic turrets on the roof and surrounded by two acres of lush grassland.

Dave let himself and Ellie in the building door and then into his flat. 'Nice of them to leave the alarm off again,' he muttered, presumably referring to his police colleagues. 'Oh well. I'll re-set it.'

Ellie gave him a nudge. 'We need to speak to your neighbour.'

'Yep. I'll just check a couple of things before we go and see Penny.'

He led Ellie to the lounge. 'There's fingerprint powder on the gloss paint, look. They should have those results now.' He opened the cupboard and a wellie fell out. Everything had been taken out and shoved back in a hurry. Coats and shoes lay on top of one another like a jumble sale stall at lunchtime.

In the kitchen, it was as Emily had described it – tidy.

'As if a killer would leave picture wire and cutters here if they'd just used them to kill someone.'

'Or blood-stained trainers in a cupboard,' said Ellie. 'You'd chuck them out, burn them or put them in the washing machine.'

'Hold on.' He opened the drawer by the kettle. 'My business cards aren't where I left them,' he said promptly, pointing at a space. 'They're always on the left here, next to the gas lighter. Not the right.'

Emily had commented on Dave's tidiness. He would know if someone had moved them.

'I reckon someone took one and planted it at Arthur's place.'

'That's one less thing to explain, then,' said Ellie.

Dave re-set the alarm, locked up and went to knock on Penny's door.

Ellie saw the muscle twitching in his cheek and knew he was nervous. She stood next to him as they waited for Penny to answer.

When she saw Dave, relief shot over her face. 'We've been very worried.' She was a petite woman around Sylvia's age and wore cream riding breeches with a quilted, mauve waistcoat over a jumper.

He introduced Ellie. 'Sorry about all the noise with the police in my flat and–'

'Don't worry at all. How are you?'

'I've been better,' he said wearily, 'but hopefully all this will be over soon. And I haven't lost family members, unlike the Durdens.' He gave her a grateful smile. 'Listen, we've got to dash but have you seen or heard anyone in my flat?'

She frowned. 'A couple of times. The police, I think.'

Dave nodded. 'You were here last week when Lloyd Durden came round and started shouting. If they need it, would you be happy to give the police a statement saying I didn't threaten him at any point?'

'Oh, yes,' she replied. 'I've already done it.'

Chapter 37

While they were waiting to meet Hayley for coffee, Sylvia rang Ralph, her ex-colleague.

She took a deep breath and asked the question she'd been putting off. 'I was wondering if you've managed to find out anything about Lloyd's time in prison?' She knew she was pushing it and, although the information could be extremely helpful, she didn't want to get Ralph into any trouble.

'Oh, no sweat,' Ralph replied down the line. 'What I did was check records with a low security classification. That way, I won't get into trouble. Obviously, I'm not meant to pass this information on, but I owe you after the glowing reference you gave me for my promotion.'

'Thank you.'

'Lloyd Durden had a number of rows. Some were with fellow inmates, others were with prison officers, doctors and staff.'

'I'm all ears.'

'What we're talking about here is who might wish him harm, yes?'

'Exactly.'

'Personally, I think it's less likely that a staff member would risk their job and livelihood by killing Lloyd, regardless of how much he may have annoyed or offended them. It's much more likely that another prisoner might have been prepared to take the risk – or been unable to stop themselves from doing so.'

'Right. Any names of anyone who's been released?'

'There are two people. However, one of them reoffended within the first week and was returned to prison by the judge.'

'Ah.'

'That leaves one. Chap called Brendan Murphy. Nasty piece of work.'

'The guy who's been on the news?'

'That's him. Numerous offences and charges. Convicted of burglary, GBH, manslaughter and blackmail. Completed his sentence and was released the week before Lloyd. From what I can see, he's breached the terms of his probation and there's a warrant out for his arrest.'

'So, if he'd wanted to hurt Lloyd, he wouldn't have had much to lose really. What's the probation term he's broken?'

'He's meant to stay within a quarter of a mile of his registered home address in Dover and he's several miles away.'

'Where?'

'In Margate. He's got family there.'

'Thanks. He's unlikely to be staying with his family as it's an obvious place for the police to look. But it's perfectly possible he's visited them, and they may know something. Changing the subject, how would I find out who visited Lloyd in prison?'

'That's something the cops will be able to find out very easily but it's much more difficult for a member of the public. I can check the records, and, depending on the security level, I might be able to find out. Not promising though...'

'That would be fabulous. Thank you. Alternatively, if I drafted an email, would you send it to the prison governor?

That way I can explain I'm trying to help my son *and* that I'm an ex-social worker.'

'Don't worry. I'll make sure he knows you're not a complete loon.' He chuckled. 'Joking, of course. Why don't we do that? Send it over and I'll forward it.'

'Will do.' A thought occurred to Sylvia. 'Hang on. You've seen this guy's records. Do you agree with the police that he's a risk to the public?'

'I'm afraid so. In my view, he's extremely dangerous.'

Chapter 38

After Sylvia's phonecall with Ralph, she went upstairs to her room and typed an email for the prison governor.

In the pub, half an hour later, Sylvia released Hayley from a hug, and gently cupped her face with her hands. She kept repeating, 'I'm so sorry. I'm so sorry.'

Hayley dabbed at her tears with a tissue. She was sitting with Sylvia, Ellie, Zoe and Dave at a table.

'I'm very relieved you've come home,' said Sylvia.

They chatted for ten minutes.

'Sorry to change the focus here, Hayles, but we need to ask you some questions.' Dave spoke with his detective inspector's voice. 'Where were you between 2.30am and 5am on Saturday morning?'

ABBA came on the pub's music system. Under the sixteenth- century building's low beams, the upbeat sound was magnified.

'At Gran's,' Hayley replied. 'In bed. Why?'

'Are you sure about that?' said Dave.

'What's going on? Why are you even asking me about this?'

'Menus,' said a waitress, tentatively, as she handed them laminated card. 'We've got hot cross buns fresh from the oven.'

Ellie took them. 'Thanks. Give us a minute, could you?'

Dave hadn't noticed her. 'Perhaps *you* can tell *us* what's going on? Starting with why you are on CCTV in the lane leading to the hare meadow with Lloyd Durden at 3am on Saturday morning.'

'I... I...' She looked from her mum to Ellie and then to her brother. 'Where are you getting this from?'

'I told you,' Dave replied. 'From CCTV. Please could you answer the question?' His tone was as impatient as his words. 'Because right now you're likely to be the police's main suspect. You were in place at the time in question, and could have had a number of motives.'

'Darling, if you lost your temper or did something rash, we'll understand.' Sylvia placed a supportive hand on her daughter's shoulder.

Dave's eyebrows shot up. He opened his mouth to speak and Ellie nudged him.

'Just tell us the truth,' said Sylvia.

Hayley pushed her mother's hand off. 'I went to meet him. Lloyd. Alright?'

'At three o'clock in the morning?' Sylvia was almost shrieking. 'Are you mad?'

'And you wonder why I didn't tell you?'

'Have you told the police you were there?' asked Dave. 'It would help my case a lot.'

Hayley stared at them all, like a rabbit in the headlights.

'What on earth were you doing, meeting him?' said Sylvia. 'You didn't have a row and kill him, did you?'

'No, I did *not*.' With that, Hayley got up. 'And that's all I'm saying on the matter. So, leave me alone. I'm going for a walk.'

Chapter 39

After Hayley's swift departure, the team were feeling downbeat. Time was running out and they needed answers.

They agreed that Ellie and Sylvia would try and speak again with Hayley in a couple of hours. Before that, they'd visit Fleming Rail Engineering to find out if they had any useful information.

Zoe had sourced the address and a map earlier in the morning, and it didn't take Ellie and Sylvia long to find the company's base in a warehouse on the Deal industrial estate.

On arrival, they blagged their way past reception and were now facing the boss in his office. Kevin Berry was a stout man in baggy, grey, suit trousers and a white shirt that hadn't seen an iron.

'We are Blix Investigators.' Sylvia put on her most authoritative air.

Kevin's eyebrows shot up. 'You here to check my payroll or something?'

'No. Don't worry we're not looking into you or your engineering company.' She smiled reassuringly. 'We're investigating the murder of Lloyd Durden a few days ago. He was found dead in the pond in the hare meadow in Lower Wootton.'

'What's that got to do with us?'

Ellie took over. 'We know your company was carrying out night-time engineering work on the railway line and we would really like to know if any of your staff saw anything. There's only one way to get to the crossing behind the meadow, where you were working in the early hours of Saturday morning, and that's along the lane which leads into the field.'

'What are you suggesting then?' asked Kevin.

'Are some of the men here who were working that night and morning?'

'Some of them are, yeah.'

'Would it be possible to get them together quickly so we can ask them?' said Sylvia. 'It's a long shot but, at the moment, my son is under suspicion, and if there's anything we can do to help him, we'd really like to. It'll literally only take a few minutes to speak to them.'

Kevin leaned over his desk and switched the warehouse tannoy on and put out a call, summoning all engineering staff to the canteen.

Ten minutes later, Sylvia and Ellie were facing a group of about twenty men.

'What's this all about then, love?' asked one.

Sylvia explained the background briefly. 'We've got four key questions. The crossing isn't accessible by vehicle so you must all have walked there. Right?'

The man nodded.

'Question one, while you were walking, there or back, did any of you see the man who's been killed? Two, did you see anyone else? Three, did you see him with anyone else? Four, did you see anyone acting suspiciously?'

'What do you mean by "suspiciously"?' asked another man.

There were titters.

Ellie resisted the urge to make a sarky comment. 'Lurking, seeming anxious, looking about, anything that might make you think the person was up to no good. The time in question is between 3am and 5am, so not many people are going to be about at that time of the morning.'

A combination of sensible and stupid questions followed. Ellie answered patiently in case any of them had information that might be helpful.

'We've printed out our contact details on these slips of paper,' she told them, 'along with the questions, so if you remember anything later, you can either call us or email. And if anyone isn't here now, who was working that shift, please pass a slip onto them.'

'I saw him,' said a quiet voice at the back of the room.

They all turned and gawped at the man who'd spoken.

'The guy who was killed. The one who's been on the news.' The man who was speaking was shorter than a lot of the other men and looked older.

'What time?'

'3.30am. I had to go back to my car. Stupidly, I'd left my phone in it and my girlfriend wasn't well that night. She's got low blood pressure and keeps passing out. I said I'd ring her at 4am to check she'd taken her medication. I told the boss.'

'He did,' said Kevin. 'I was on site myself.'

'I was there and back in about fifteen minutes,' the eye-witness continued. 'And I passed a bloke.'

'What was he doing?'

'Rushing, like he was late. And looking over his shoulder as if he was worried someone would see him.'

'Did he meet anyone? Or talk to anyone on the phone?'

'Dunno. I just saw him rushing on the lane towards the meadow. Halfway along, I had to turn off to get to the crossing, so I didn't follow him the whole way.'

Sylvia got the witness' contact details in case they needed to ask him any further questions. She thanked the men, and the manager.

'There are around five men who aren't here, who were working that night, so I'll let them know,' Kevin told them. 'We also had two inspectors visit the crossing that night. I'll ask them too. See if they saw anything.' He paused, shaking his head. 'My wife likes walking in that meadow in the summer. And my daughter cuts through it on her way home from the station sometimes. They're both scared to go there now. We need to catch whoever did this. Get everyone feeling safe again.'

Chapter 40

The woman's voice on the phone was high pitched and she was gabbling.

Ellie switched the loudspeaker on so Sylvia could hear too. They'd just got back into the jeep.

'... and he's been in our barn. Goodness knows how long he's been here. I found an old blanket, so it looks like he's been sleeping here. Anything could've happened...' She broke off with a terrified gasp.

'Is that Mrs Gardner, from the white house in the lane?' Ellie asked, trying to keep her voice calm.

'That's me. Left cigarette butts and matches everywhere, he did. Could've set light to the place.'

Sylvia clamped her hand over her mouth.

'Must've been what spooked our dog the night that poor chap was killed,' continued Mrs Gardner. 'My husband and I are terrified. We've seen the warnings from the police on the news. About him being violent. Telling people not to approach him.'

'I can quite understand you being scared. Can I just clarify: are we talking about the man with the tattoos? Brendan Murphy?'

'Yes. That's him. I've locked all the doors and phoned the police.'

Ellie calmed her down, made sure she knew what she needed to do and rang off. She turned to Sylvia. 'It's all happening now. We're getting close. I can sense it. Can't you?'

Sylvia looked like she was about to burst. 'Ellie, *the dog*.'

'What dog?'

'When Mrs Gardner mentioned their dog getting spooked in the early hours, it reminded me. Except I didn't think anything of it at the time.'

'Any chance you could explain what you're talking about?'

'On the CCTV at the building site, the camera showed a dog chasing a rabbit in the field next to the hare meadow. What was the dog doing out at that time? And where was its owner? She paused. 'Zoe's got a copy of the CCTV on a USB stick so we can check, but I'm pretty sure I know whose dog it was. Lydia Durden's.'

Chapter 41

'We had a feeling you'd be here,' said Ellie gently. 'Are you OK?'

Hayley shook her head. She was sitting on the grass in the hare meadow by the pond.

Ellie and Sylvia sat down near her.

'No one wants to upset you, Hayley, love,' said Sylvia. 'I'm sorry if you think we're having a go at you, or ganging up on you. None of us has a clue what's going on, and the situation with Lloyd and Arthur's murder is obviously very serious.'

Hayley nodded.

'If you feel up to talking, we'd like to listen,' Sylvia continued. 'We're worried you're in trouble and we want to help. All of us, including your brother.'

Hayley snorted. 'Yeah, right. All he's ever done is ruin my life.'

'What d'you mean?'

The comment had registered with Ellie too.

'Forget it.'

'Well then, can you explain why you wanted to see Lloyd on Saturday morning?'

'I wanted to talk to him.'

'What about?'

'It was personal.'

'You'll need to elaborate, I'm afraid,' said Sylvia. 'If not to us, to the police. Lloyd's death is a murder investigation. Dave is currently one of the police suspects. If you were the last person to see him, or one of them, you need to explain what you were doing.'

Hayley stuck her nose in the air and jutted her chin defiantly.

'Was he alive when you left him?' asked Ellie softly.

'Of course he was. You don't think I killed him, do you?'

'We have no idea what to think,' said Sylvia. 'You come back to the village out of the blue, turn up at Mum's house, don't tell anyone else that you're here, and then you sneak off to meet the man who got you pregnant when you were in the sixth form the night before he's due to get married. Which part of that doesn't raise questions?'

Hurt spread across Hayley's face. Tears welled in her eyes. 'You don't have to be aggressive about it.'

'Well, could you answer the question then, please?' said Sylvia. 'What did you go to talk to him about?'

'If you must know, he wanted to apologise. I didn't tell anyone where I was going because I didn't want anyone to know. And, to be honest, I wasn't sure myself what his motivation was.' She fiddled with her necklace. 'You probably don't know this, but he contacted me several times after sixth form and I wasn't sure whether this was going to be similar to that: him wanting to see if he could twist me round his little finger again, that sort of thing.'

'Sweetie,' whispered Sylvia, 'why would you want to put yourself through that?'

'To show him he couldn't do it anymore. That I wasn't his for the taking like I was back then.'

Ellie put her hand on Sylvia's, keen to keep Hayley talking. 'And how did it go?'

'Actually, to his credit, I don't know whether being in prison changed him, or whether somebody had had a word with him, but he actually apologised for messing me about so spectacularly, and for dumping me when I got pregnant.'

'Let me get this straight,' said Sylvia. 'You met him in the hare meadow. He apologised to you for his past behaviour and then you went home.'

'Pretty much,' Hayley replied. 'I know it sounds ridiculous. As I said, that's why I kept it to myself.'

'Lloyd did know you'd got pregnant in the sixth form, didn't he?' asked Ellie.

Hayley nodded. 'He didn't want anything to do with me. Told me to get rid of it.' She closed her eyes as she said the two sentences, and a large tear escaped and ran down her cheek.

'Oh, sweetie. That must've been so painful. Is that what you did?'

She shook her head, both hands cupping her face. 'I had a miscarriage two weeks before our A-levels.' She stared at them, pain etched on every feature, her voice a squeak. 'I was still deciding what to do.'

They were all silent for a few moments.

'I could throttle your father for not telling me about this,' said Sylvia finally. 'I could have supported you. Looked after you.'

'You did, Mum. You just didn't know it. Dad and I told you I had period pain. You brought me home-made fish fingers in bed – because they're my favourite – and lots of lovely cake. And a hot water bottle when I was on the sofa.'

'Hayles, darling.' Sylvia swooped her daughter up in a hug.

A few moments later, they continued asking Hayley questions.

'You said you met Lloyd at 3am, right?' said Ellie. 'Why then? Why not at a reasonable time rather than in the middle of the night?'

'He said he had wanted to suggest it earlier in the week but kept talking himself out of it. But really wanted to see me before he got married so messaged me at the last minute. It was then or not at all.'

'How did he know you were back in Lower Wootton?'

'I told him.'

'Why?'

'I don't know. I've felt so confused lately. I heard he was getting married and wasn't sure how I felt.'

'Did you tell him you were back hoping he'd suggest meeting, then?' Ellie was trying to get inside her sister-in-law's mind.

Hayley shrugged.

'This is important,' said Ellie, trying to remain patient. 'Where were you when you parted ways?'

'Here, by the pond. I didn't want him walking me back to Gran's, or walking me anywhere, because I didn't want anyone to see us together. So, I said goodbye and left.'

'And – to be absolutely clear – you left him *here*?'

'Yes.'

'What time?'

'Ten minutes later. Literally.'

'Did you see anyone else? Here in the field, or in the lane?'

'No.'

'Are you sure?'

'Positive.'

'Did he say he was meeting anyone else?'

'He said he was meeting Dave.'

'In the middle of the night? Did you believe him?'

She shrugged.

'Why would he be meeting Dave? Lloyd had been round to his flat a few days earlier, drunk, hurling accusations and threats. Dave told him to sling his hook and not come back.'

'Dunno.'

'Why would Dave then arrange to meet him again? Your brother had no desire to see him the first time.'

A sinking feeling crept over Ellie. 'What if Lloyd had lured Dave to the meadow to get his revenge on him?'

'I suppose they could've had a fight,' said Hayley. 'What if it got out of control and Dave ended up losing his temper again? And this time, instead of breaking Lloyd's ribs, he ended up killing him?'

Ellie looked at Hayley, trying to take in what she was saying. Did she really think her brother was capable of murder? Did she believe what she was saying or was she just churning out the suggestion to deflect attention?

Hayley continued. 'I haven't been around to know what's gone on between them all these years. I'm just telling you what Lloyd said. That's what you asked me.'

As Hayley was speaking, Ellie had been trying to put her finger on why Hayley was angry with Dave. Her "all he's ever done is ruin my life" comment suggested she was deeply unhappy with how Dave had acted. Did that refer to him punching Lloyd and pushing him down the stairs? Hurting him and splitting them up? If she was in love with Lloyd, it might've been hard for Hayley to accept that Dave had been trying to protect her.

'And Lloyd definitely said "Dave"?' asked Sylvia. 'It wasn't another name that sounds similar?'

'Like what? No. I didn't press him as to which Dave. He just said "Dave", like we both knew who he meant.'

'Or that's what he *wanted* you to think, more like,' said Sylvia.

'Did Lloyd say *why* he was meeting him?'

'No. And I didn't ask. I just wanted to get home.'

'Sorry to keep banging on about this, but didn't you think it was odd that the night before his wedding, Lloyd arranged to meet both you and your brother?'

'I suppose a bit, but I didn't really think that much about it. He apologised to me and that was it. There weren't any ego games or shenanigans after that, so in a way his request to meet was authentic. I think I sort of assumed he had a good reason to want to meet Dave.'

It was all a bit of a ramble.

'I knew there'd been bad blood between them ever since sixth form,' Hayley continued, 'so I guess I thought he was going to apologise to Dave as well. But, like I said, I really didn't give it that much thought. It wasn't easy for me to meet up with him after all this time and I was very anxious about it. I'm afraid I thought mainly about myself.'

She stared at them.

'You'll need to tell the police all this,' said Ellie.

She nodded. 'Am I the last person to have seen Lloyd alive, then?'

Chapter 42

The three sleuths were all back at the windmill for an urgent team meeting. Dave had joined them.

Ellie kicked off. 'OK, so what's changed and who are our suspects now?'

'I'm confident Hayley isn't responsible,' said Sylvia, 'despite her being in the hare meadow with Lloyd at 3am.' She shook her head in exasperation. 'I still can't believe she was so stupid.'

'She seems to want to suggest I killed him,' said Dave. 'I'm not sure she's thinking straight at the moment.'

'I agree she's off-kilter.' Ellie had been trying to weigh this up since they spoke to Hayley. 'And I cannot figure out if she hates Lloyd or still loves him... But – murder? Surely no.'

'Didn't we all think she'd moved on?' asked Sylvia. 'It's so sad.'

'But if he'd been stirring her up?' said Ellie. 'I don't think she'd go to the meadow for an apology at 3am if she was indifferent to him.'

'I agree,' said Zoe. 'The psychologist on *RealCrimeTV* calls it "enmeshed".'

'That's *exactly* what it is,' said Sylvia. 'She hasn't separated herself from Lloyd cheating on her and getting her pregnant.'

'Let's consider who else is capable of killing him,' said Ellie.

'We know Brendan Murphy is in the area,' said Zoe. 'He's been seen in the lane by the hare meadow in the early hours of Saturday morning. That puts him on the spot at the critical time. He had lots of run-ins with Lloyd in prison, and the Gardners are convinced he's been kipping in their barn.'

'What doesn't make sense about him, though,' said Sylvia, 'is if he killed Lloyd, he must know he'll be going straight back to prison. No?'

'Perhaps he's a psychopath and doesn't care?' Zoe suggested. 'Literally all he wants is revenge.'

'Sylvia, you mentioned that Lydia's dog was in the field next to the hare meadow at 3am,' said Ellie. 'She must've been with it. Could she have arranged to meet Lloyd? Revenge for Joan. We'll need to speak to her again.'

'I've talked to Lydia and I find her nice but a bit elusive,' replied Sylvia. 'And vague. It worries me that she might be capable of convincing herself that Lloyd deserved to die.'

'What about Dr Peters? Could he have killed Lloyd?'

'He's my GP,' said Zoe. 'There's no doubt he despised Lloyd, but he'd lose his career and the life he's created.'

'Ian Chapman's wife says he was with her all night,' said Ellie. 'But the alibi of a spouse won't carry much weight with the police.'

'And we were so bowled over by what Belinda told us,' said Sylvia, 'we completely forgot to ask her where she was on Friday evening and afterwards.'

Ellie put her hand on Sylvia's wrist.

'What about the railway engineer's testimony?' said Dave, who'd been listening eagerly. 'He said he'd seen Brendan in the lane, didn't he?'

'Actually, you know what?' Ellie sat up. 'I've just realised. He said he'd seen the guy from the TV. Both Lloyd and Brendan have been on the TV. How do we know which one he was talking about?'

Dave came in. 'And if he saw Lloyd, so what? We know he was in the hare meadow because he got killed there.'

'He gave me us number,' said Ellie. 'I'll call him.' She got up and fetched her phone and his number from her bag. Dialled.

'Hello?'

'Is that Darren? It's Ellie Blix. We spoke to you at–'

'It is. How can I help?'

In the background, Ellie heard the clunking of metal, the beeping of a reversing vehicle and a man yelling.

'We realised the police have been talking about two men on the news recently. One is the man who's been killed, Lloyd Durden. The other is a convict who's broken the terms of his probation. Could I clarify, please – which one did you see in the lane?'

'The one with–'

'No, Reeby. *Leave.*' Zoe leaped off her chair and crawled under the table. 'He's got the box of chocolates Finn gave me. Looks like he's wolfed the lot.' She extracted the plastic tray from Rebus' mouth. 'We need to get him to the vet for an emetic. Quickly.'

Chapter 43

There were only two customers in the waiting room at the vet's when Ellie and Zoe arrived with Rebus, who by now was panting.

It was a large space, separated into an area for cats and one for dogs. There were racks of leaflets, and pet toys and accessories on display.

'Are your pets here for emergency appointments?' Zoe asked them. 'Our dog's just eaten chocolate.'

'Go ahead,' said a woman with a black spaniel. 'He's only having a nail trim.'

The owner of an unhappy cat said, 'Mine's getting a booster.'

They checked Rebus in and waited impatiently for the vet to come out and call them. Within a few minutes, a veterinary nurse came out.

'Hi. I'm Laura. I'm going to check Rebus' weight. We'll need it for the emetic. Do you want to bring him through?'

He was quickly weighed and seen by the vet. Given a drug to make him cough up the chocolate before his stomach absorbed it.

Fifteen minutes later, Ellie, Zoe and Rebus were in a side room, with the nurse, waiting for a poorly Rebus to recover enough to go home.

'You must know Amy, then?' Ellie asked, making conversation.

Laura nodded. 'Great laugh, she is. I'll be sad when she and her boyfriend move away. The Lake District is going to be very different from having her round the corner, here in the village.'

'But she won't be moving now, will she?'

And hadn't Amy said they'd booked the Lake District for their honeymoon but were planning to settle in the village?

Laura frowned. 'What d'you mean? They're buying a bed and breakfast, she said.' She took Rebus' temperature and heart rate. 'He's good to go. Should be absolutely fine now. May be a bit dozy for a few hours, so keep an eye on him and make sure he has plenty of water.'

'Thank you,' said Zoe. 'I feel so bad that he got my chocolates. I thought I'd put them out of his reach but obviously not. We've had kittens staying. Reckon they've taught him bad habits.'

They laughed.

Ellie couldn't help thinking what a shame it was that Amy and Lloyd hadn't managed to get away and fulfil their dream. But more, that Laura didn't seem to have heard the news about Lloyd's murder.

'I'm not sure Amy was happy with her old boyfriend,' said Laura, 'but she seems keen on this one. I'll miss her, of course.'

'You two were at the fancy dress party in the pub last week, weren't you?' Zoe nudged her mother who stopped stroking Rebus' head.

'Yes,' replied Laura. 'Were you there?'

'Only briefly and not for the party. Your costumes were brilliant. Mum, you'd have appreciated them. Amy was dressed as a ballerina and Laura was–'

'... a jockey.'

'That sounds fun,' said Ellie. 'I love fancy dress. Did you take any photos?'

'A few. Hold on.' Laura grabbed her phone from the table at the side of the room and swiped it into action. 'Here we go. This was before we started on the tequila shots.' She held out her screen for them to see.

In the photo, Laura looked very different from the vet nurse in scrubs who was with them now. Her hair was in a ballerina's topknot. She wore a white leotard with matching tights and tutu. Next to her, holding a glass of fizz and a riding crop, was Amy, in white breeches, a pink, silk jacket and a helmet with a pink cover. Both wore glamorous make-up.

'I hope she can get away from this place,' said Laura as she flicked through a few more selfies and showed them. 'Make a fresh start. If anyone deserves to be happy, it's Amy.'

And, with those few comments, and Laura's photos, the final penny dropped into place amongst all the others.

The case finally made sense.

Lloyd's murder and Arthur's.

'We need to get everyone together before anyone else is hurt,' Ellie whispered to Zoe. 'I know who the killer is.'

Chapter 44

At the windmill, Ellie updated Sylvia, Zoe and Dave on who the murderer was, and issued instructions.

'Amy's struggling at the moment so we'll meet at her place.' She glanced at Dave. 'Can you get DS Carmichael? If she's coming in her own car, could you pick up Sarge and Nick?'

'Sure,' he replied.

She turned to Sylvia. 'Could you collect Belinda? And Lydia and Dr Peters from the surgery? And ask Leonard to meet us at Amy's?'

'No problem.'

'Zo, lovey, could you get Laura from the vet's, and Sally from home?'

Just over an hour later, the lounge of Amy's flat was packed. Lydia, Ian and Belinda were huddled together by the fireplace. Sarge was on a chair nearby with Sean standing behind him. Amy and her mother were on the sofa with the cat. Dave and Nick stood at the back of the room by the door, with DS Carmichael and Dr Peters. Hayley and Finn were with the vicar and Laura, the veterinary nurse, next to the door.

Ellie always felt conflicted before these gatherings. Nervous. Worried about the implications for everyone involved of identifying the killer. But, at the same time, she also felt galvanised to finish what they'd started; to bring what closure they could, and to return the village to a sense of safety and stability.

She stood next to Sylvia and Zoe, facing everyone. Cleared her throat and took a swig of water.

'This case was challenging from the start because there were so many potential suspects; people Lloyd had fallings-out with or antagonised, either as a result of his campaign to have the speed limit lifted in the village or as a result of Joan's tragic death. However, once we started talking to witnesses, we realised that there were a few other categories of people where suspects might also be likely.'

Hayley was chewing her nails.

'As soon as the news of Lloyd's death surfaced,' Ellie continued, 'we knew it was going to be an upsetting investigation for everyone, largely because Joan's death was only two-and-a-bit years ago.' She looked in Ian's direction. 'Lloyd was released from prison and we are all still healing.'

'Too right,' muttered Ian.

Sylvia spoke now. 'We quickly realised, however, that some of the key players were not actually as they seemed. We discovered secrets and lies going back decades, as much within our own family as within other people's. None of it has been easy, and our conclusions certainly will not be either.'

A chill went round the room.

She glanced at Ellie, her face full of apprehension. 'We didn't want to take on this investigation and wouldn't have if it hadn't been for my son's arrest and how distressed he was about it.'

Dave gave a brief nod.

'Ian, for a while we weren't sure whether you had played a role, and it was evident to everybody that you had a clear and compelling motive.'

He looked sheepish.

'Lydia, you've been convinced that you were going to be set up for your brother's murder. However, as soon as your father was killed, we believed the same person was responsible for his death as your brother's, and we couldn't see any reason why you would be motivated to take the life of your own father.' She softened her voice. 'He had always favoured your brother, and no doubt his unwavering support for him after Joan's death will have caused you pain. But would you have killed him for that?'

'Never,' replied Lydia, through sniffs. 'My poor dad.' She blew her nose.

'However, perhaps you can explain why your dog was seen in the field next to the hare meadow in the early hours of Saturday morning? I assume you were with him?'

'B-b-barney was off the lead, and he'd scrambled through the hedge along the lane and gone after a rabbit. I couldn't sleep – blasted insomnia – and we'd gone out for a walk. A regular occurrence for us these days, sadly. As a few of the villagers will no doubt confirm,' she said, looking in Leonard's direction.

'You do realise this puts you on the spot at the time of Lloyd's death?'

She nodded. 'And as much as, in m-m-my mind, I've wished Lloyd harm for what he did to Joan, I did not kill him. As you said, I've been convinced I was going to be set up for this crime but, actually, I realised how ridiculous that is. Apart from the fact I took the dog out in the early hours, there will be *no* evidence against me. Because I didn't kill him, and I certainly did not kill Dad.'

Sylvia thanked her and turned to Ellie, gesturing for her to continue.

'Hayley, we are aware this has been a traumatic time for you,' Ellie said. 'I didn't know about Dave's fight with Lloyd when Lloyd cheated on you, and neither Dave nor I knew that you'd got pregnant. I can only imagine what that must have been like for you, and I'm so sorry I wasn't there to support you and look after you. We all wish we could have protected you more.' She glanced at Sylvia and Dave. 'It has, however, been of great concern to us that you chose now to return to Lower Wootton. With Lloyd's release from prison, and imminent marriage, it's difficult to believe those are coincidental.'

Hayley shuddered.

'In addition, some of your decisions and actions have been highly dubious. It was you who was following Lloyd, wasn't it?'

She nodded.

'Why?'

'I wanted to see for myself whether he really loved her.' Hayley glanced over at Amy. 'But I stopped after a couple of days because I quickly realised that neither of them loved the other at all.'

Amy looked at her mum. 'What did she say?'

Ellie continued. 'Amy, we know how upsetting Lloyd's death is for you, doubly so because it occurred the day the two of you were due to get married.'

Amy sniffed and dabbed her nose with a tissue.

'We've been moved by your grief and your tears.'

'Thank you.'

'There are a couple of questions I'd like to ask, however, if that's OK.'

She nodded.

'It must have been terribly difficult to be separated from the man you loved when he was in prison. Did you find your visits a comfort?'

'To be honest, without them, I don't think we would have got through. I've loved Lloyd since I was a teenager. It's a long time to wait for someone. I just can't believe that we got so close to getting married and being together forever.'

'With a bond such as yours, I can see why you both made each other the benefactors in your wills. That must have been a comfort too, was it?'

Amy sniffed again. 'That was Lloyd's suggestion. He owned a house and he wanted to be sure that, if anything happened to him, I would be taken care of. I have no idea of the value. It's probably very little once his mortgage is paid off.'

'Of course. Although he doesn't have a mortgage. He owns the house outright. Didn't you know?' Ellie was waiting for confirmation on this but wanted to see what Amy's response would be.

'No-o.' Her eyebrows rose in surprise. 'I didn't like to ask.'

'It's always reassuring when we can get legal work done by someone we know and trust, isn't it? We've got an excellent solicitor in the village, William Hardman. He's done all my legal work, and my family's. I'm surprised you didn't use him. How did you come to know Harold Bains?'

'Lloyd introduced me. They knew each other through work.'

'And neither your fiancé nor Mr Bains informed you Lloyd didn't have a mortgage?'

She shook her head.

'That's OK. It'll be easy enough for the police to check with Bains & Broad, Solicitors.' She paused. 'What about Brendan Murphy? How did you come to know him?'

A frown flickered across Amy's features. 'Also through Lloyd.'

'Do you know each other well?'

She shook her head and her curls fluttered. 'Oh no. Not at all. He was just a mate of Lloyd's.'

'I think I'm correct in saying the two men met in prison. That's right, isn't it?'

'Uh-huh.'

'Did you visit Brendan in prison too?'

'No. As I said, I don't really know him.'

'It's just that the prison governor confirmed to us that you only went to see Lloyd once, and that was when he needed to sign his new will, making you his sole beneficiary. That's correct, isn't it?' She paused and waited to see how the question landed with Amy.

She frowned. 'What? No, that's not right. I visited Lloyd loads. Probably every month to six weeks. Something like that. The governor must have got his records wrong.'

'We wondered that too. In fact, so much so that we asked him to double check. And his clerk reconfirmed: you made *one* trip to see Lloyd, to get the will signed.'

'No, no. That's not correct.'

'He also said you made numerous other visits though. Could you tell us who you were going to see?'

'No-one. Just Lloyd.'

'Why then don't the prison records reflect that?'

'Someone must've made an error.' She opened her eyes little- girl wide and surveyed the room. 'That's all I can suggest.'

Ellie held up a printout of what the clerk had sent them. 'The records show you went to see Brendan Murphy.'

'Well, it's not true. Where is the governor getting this from? It's complete rubbish. He must have got things mixed up and thought I visited Brendan a lot when it was Lloyd. He just made a mistake. That's all.'

'Well, the police will be able to get Mr Murphy to confirm his side of the story.' She checked her watch. 'He should be reaching the custody suite around about now. DS Carmichael picked him up in Margate earlier.'

'I can confirm that's correct,' came DS Carmichael's voice from the back of the room.

'What?' Amy quickly checked her reaction. 'Oh. Thank goodness he'll be back behind bars.' She fanned her face.

'I'm sorry, Amy,' Ellie continued. 'There's no mistake. You went to see Mr Murphy regularly. It's not as if somebody completes a visitors' book by hand weeks afterwards and has to rely on memory. All prison visits are logged electronically when they are booked, and the software includes details of the time of arrival and departure, and who came. You went several times on your own to see Brendan Murphy. Once to see Lloyd. Doesn't that strike you as a bit strange? Especially when you say you loved Lloyd such a lot.'

'Yes, it does, because it's not true.'

'OK. Let's come back to that and move on for now. Did you know that Lloyd had cheated on Hayley with you at school?'

'No?'

'And that, having then dumped Hayley for you, he then cheated on *you* with *her*?'

'No. But what's this got to do with anything?'

'That's exactly what we've been trying to figure out. If you had to guess, what would you say?'

She blushed.

'So, are you claiming you didn't know Lloyd got Hayley Blix pregnant then?'

'I most certainly did not.' Amy shot Dave's sister a dirty look. 'How could I have known? I had no idea that Lloyd and Hayley had any kind of relationship at all, beyond going to the same school and living in the same village.'

'In that case, how do you explain a witness overhearing you and Lloyd having an argument in which you raised the subject of him getting someone pregnant?'

'I don't. I can't, because it never happened.'

Ellie addressed her best friend. 'Sal, could you outline for us exactly what you heard, please?'

Sally stepped forward and faced the group. 'For a couple of years my partner and I were involved with the village amateur dramatics group. We didn't have any acting ambitions – or talent, frankly – so we helped out with the set building, making costumes, ticket sales, publicity. One evening, at a rehearsal, Lloyd turned up, drunk as usual, and proceeded to have a blazing row with Amy in the ladies' toilets at the community centre, where the show was being held. She was a member of the cast. I had a bad cold that day and had come out without my tissues, so I went in to grab a handful of toilet roll to blow my nose on. That's when I heard their argument.'

'You're lying. Or it was another couple you heard rowing.' Amy looked round the room to see what sort of reaction this was getting. 'She's making it up. Lloyd never went to the community centre when we were rehearsing.'

'I can assure you I'm not making it up,' said Sally. 'What I heard was you confronting Lloyd with having got someone pregnant when they were in the sixth form. You were hopping mad because you'd only just found out.'

'Absolute rubbish.'

'And I know it was the two of you because I saw you both. I was embarrassed and hid in one of the cubicles. Had a quick peek though, to check who it was. Although, from the conversation, I had no doubt.'

Ellie smiled gratefully at Sally. 'What was Lloyd's response?'

'He denied it,' said Sally.

'Did she mention, during the row, how she'd found out about the pregnancy?'

'Yes. Through her aunt, Belinda. It was how she opened the discussion: "I've just heard from Belinda that you got some girl pregnant when she was in the sixth form".'

'Thank you.' Ellie turned now to Belinda. 'Could you confirm – did you tell Amy?'

'Sorry, Amy,' she said, looking tearfully at her niece. 'I did. I thought she should know. But I didn't say who it was.'

'You knew though?'

'Yes. It was Hayley Blix.'

'Thank you. I have some other questions for you in a minute but want to go back to Amy.'

Belinda nodded.

'Amy, you were seen with a man in the graveyard by the compost heap. That was Brendan Murphy, wasn't it? Lloyd's mate from prison.'

'Pardon me?'

'You were with Brendan Murphy. The ex-convict.'

'If I can just step in here,' said Dave. 'Brendan Murphy is not just an ex-convict. Until an hour or so ago, he was wanted by police for having broken the terms of his probation. I don't wish to scare you all by listing the crimes he was convicted of, and those he's been charged with in the past, but suffice it to say, he's a violent, dangerous man. I'm very relieved he's back in custody.'

Whispers went round the room.

Ellie focused on Amy again. 'What I find strange about this is that, despite Brendan Murphy's known offences – and predilection for violence – you embarked on a romantic relationship with him behind Lloyd's back.'

'Hold on.' Amy stood up again. 'Where are you getting this from? It's just more lies and defamation.'

'Actually, a witness saw you and Brendan snogging regularly on the bench in the graveyard. You dropped your lipstick.' She held it up. 'The one I've seen you wearing in at least *two* photos recently. Are you asking us to believe you weren't having an affair with him?'

'Amy!' her mother shouted. 'I told you to leave Lloyd, but you never listen. If only you'd finished with him, this would never have happened.'

There was a deathly hush in the room.

Everyone stared at the woman in a baggy jumper and tracksuit bottoms, glasses hanging on a cord round her neck.

'Oh, shut up, Mum,' Amy spat the words, eyes narrowed in anger. 'She's always exaggerating. And I can only think your witness needs his or her eyes testing. I haven't been "snogging" anyone. I'm not fifteen.' She shifted her expression, affecting sobs. 'I can't believe people are so quick to judge, to accuse, to point fingers. I was due to get married on Saturday, for goodness' sake.' She took a tissue from her pocket and blew her nose again loudly.

Ellie waited. She'd expected exactly this reaction. Indignation and counter-accusations.

'How long did you act with the Wootton Amateur Dramatics Group?'

'About five years.'

'Considerable *dramatic* experience, then.'

Amy muttered under her breath.

'Returning to the witness who saw you and Mr Murphy, I've no doubt the police will be able to test his eyesight. However, we've shown him photographs and he is one hundred per cent certain they show you and Brendan.'

She didn't mention that Sarge and Sean had been planting bulbs in the flowerbed only feet away, close enough to practically touch the young couple. Sarge was vulnerable and Ellie didn't want to reveal his identity to Amy and put him in danger. The police could take his evidence and keep him safe.

'More fabrication.'

'We'll let the police be the judge of that, shall we? Perhaps the two of you were so wrapped up in your conversation – and snogging – that you didn't notice who was around you. Rather careless, wouldn't you say?'

Amy's mum had her fingers over her mouth.

'There was no carelessness,' said Amy. 'No snogging. No affair. I was meeting the owner of another veterinary practice to discuss a job.'

Someone snorted, and Amy must have realised how ridiculous her explanation sounded.

'OK, we might not have chosen the best place to meet,' Amy continued, her voice shaking a little now, 'but my priority was making sure my current employer didn't find out that I was exploring other opportunities. A promotion, in this case.'

Ellie suppressed a laugh. 'All of which could've been achieved by meeting this person at his practice. Much less likelihood of being seen there, surely? Whereas, meeting as you did, on a bench at the back of the graveyard... It suggests something completely different, doesn't it? However, let's give you the benefit of the doubt on this one and move on.'

Amy frowned, confused.

'If someone had heard your conversation with your "vet colleague", what do you think they might have heard? A discussion about pay and holiday entitlement, for example?'

'Er... yes, exactly that. Plus my current notice period and when I could start. Bonuses. That sort of thing.'

'And what would you say if I told you we *have* a witness, who says you told them about a very different plan – to run a bed and breakfast in the Lake District?'

'I'd say you're making it up. Lloyd and I were going to have our honeymoon *there* and settle *here* in the village. With our families.'

'This person has confirmed they're happy to give evidence to the police. So, I'll read a brief extract from their email to me earlier.' She held up an A4 PDF document. '"Ms Hardcastle told me she and her boyfriend, Brendan, were–"'

'Nope,' Amy interrupted. 'Never said that to anyone. For the simple reason Brendan isn't – and never was – my boyfriend.'

Ellie ignored her. '"Ms Hardcastle told me she and her boyfriend, Brendan, were going to move to the Lake District and buy and run a bed and breakfast."'

'You should've left him.' Amy's mother was on her feet, wagging her finger. 'It was always going to end in tragedy, thinking you could use his inheritance money and get away with it. This isn't how I brought you up.'

'Oh, sit down, Mum.'

'I'm ashamed of you. *Ashamed*, do you hear?'

Ellie waited for Mrs Hardcastle to finish, then addressed the next witness. 'Laura, when you initially told me Amy had talked about buying a B&B with her boyfriend, I assumed you meant Lloyd. Could you confirm, please, what your understanding was of Ms Hardcastle's plans?'

'Sure.' Laura's voice was croaky. 'I've worked with Amy for two years at the local vet's. In that time, she has consistently referred to Brendan as her "boyfriend" and to Lloyd as her "ex-boyfriend".'

'It's not true.' Amy's voice was quieter.

'The bed and breakfast,' Ellie continued, 'that you and Brendan were going to run in the Lake District, with *Lloyd's inheritance money.* Once you'd got Brendan to kill him.'

There was a collective gasp in the room.

'Because that's what this was about, wasn't it? Getting your hands on Lloyd's money. That's why you couldn't do what your mother suggested and simply leave Lloyd. Because, that way, you wouldn't inherit a penny.'

DS Carmichael stepped forward. 'Except, you never really planned to go through with the B&B thing, did you, Amy? Because you dumped Brendan this morning. Told him you were too grief-stricken to leave the village.' She looked round the room. 'Isn't the truth that you just used Brendan to get rid of Lloyd, so you could get your hands on his inheritance money? He was just a means to an end for you.'

Amy's mother let out a sob. 'I told you to call it off.' Her voice was a strangle of emotions. 'To do the right thing. If only you'd done what I said. Poor Arthur would still be alive too.'

Dave and Ellie caught each other's eye.

'I'll look forward to seeing your evidence then, DS Carmichael.' Amy managed a sneer, but Ellie could see her bravado was failing. 'You won't find the testimony of a jilted man very reliable. It'll simply look like he's saying anything to get back at me.'

'I doubt you'll find that evidence is lacking against Mr Murphy,' Ellie told her. 'However, let's look at the other aspects of the case. See what evidence they present, shall we?'

'Whatever.'

'What about the bloody trainers and picture wire that were left in DI Blix's flat? Mr Murphy has been arrested numerous times for breaking and entering. He also has a lucrative business, which he resurrected when he left prison, installing security devices and protection equipment. And one of DI Blix's neighbours has testified to seeing a man matching Mr Murphy's description entering Mr Blix's flat. Dressed as a workman.'

'I don't know why you're asking me about this. It's him you need to speak to.'

'The reason is, the police will be able to check all your communication devices and data, *and* Mr Murphy's. Your bank accounts and transactions. Are you telling me they won't find *any evidence* of the two of you planning this?'

Amy flushed red.

'We know you persuaded Mr Murphy to kill Lloyd for you. The same witness who saw the two of you on the bench in the graveyard heard some of your conversations.

And this person didn't hear anything about contract terms or holiday allowances.' She got her phone out and swiped the screen. 'What they heard was you saying to Mr Murphy, "We can use the money to start our new life in the Lake District."'

Ellie looked over at Sean. 'Can you confirm, please, this is what you heard?'

'Those exact words,' he said.

'No,' Amy stated, but her defiance was slipping.

Ellie held up her phone. 'I put it to you that you instructed Mr Murphy to kill Lloyd's father too, and to leave DI Blix's business card on the coffee table, in the hope it would incriminate him. You see, Arthur Durden rang me not long before he was killed. He said he knew who'd killed his son and wanted to tell me. Except you and Brendan Murphy silenced him before he was able to.'

'No-o.' Amy was trembling.

'You seem to be saying that a lot. You're going to find it hard to keep up. I want now to return to your aunt.' She glanced at Belinda. 'You told me you had a private investigator following Lloyd. You also said he was someone your niece recommended. Could you tell us who it was, please?'

Belinda was shaking her head in shame, her eyes closed. 'It was Brendan Murphy.'

'How long did he provide this service?'

'Until I saw him on the news.'

'Did you tell the police he'd been working for you?'

'No, I didn't. When I dismissed him, he took off in a temper, so I didn't know where he was. I confronted Amy and told her to come clean about whatever her involvement was with Brendan, and said if she didn't, I would tell the police what I knew. His website looked convincing. Stupidly, I didn't take up references or run checks before I employed him.'

Amy was silent now, biting her lip.

'And yet, Amy, you claim not to know Mr Murphy.'

'I said I knew him a bit, through Lloyd.'

'Did you get the impression that your niece "knew him a bit"?' Ellie said to Belinda.

'Absolutely not. I knew something was going on between them. I hoped it meant she was going to dump Lloyd, so I stupidly didn't ask enough questions. It was only when I saw him on the TV news that I began to realise I'd made a mistake.'

Amy began to cry.

'The point is, Amy, you knew Mr Murphy well. You've been seen kissing him. You've been heard talking together about your plans to spend Lloyd's inheritance money. And you told a colleague you and Mr Murphy were going to buy a B&B and run it together. It's time to come clean. You asked Brendan Murphy to kill Lloyd and Arthur Durden, didn't you? You used him to get your hands on Lloyd's money?'

'OK,' she said finally. 'I admit we plotted to kill Lloyd. And had to kill his father. But it was *not* my idea. Brendan saw me visiting Lloyd and bombarded me with love letters. He suggested getting rid of Lloyd and moving away together.'

Ellie wasn't surprised to hear this from Amy. 'The police will need to see those letters. I take it you still have them.'

'I... I...'

'You don't, do you? Because it was your idea, not Mr Murphy's. And with Mr Murphy now in custody, it'll be interesting to see what he says about any letters. But you've admitted you and he plotted the murders together. So, time's up, Amy. You're busted.'

Amy looked down at the ground. 'OK. But it was only because Lloyd was such a–'

'Amy Hardcastle,' DS Carmichael stepped forward and approached Amy, 'I am arresting you for the murder of Lloyd and Arthur Durden under joint enterprise. You do not have to say anything, but it may harm your defence if you do not mention when questioned something that you later rely on in court. Anything you do say may be given in evidence.'

Chapter 45
SATURDAY

It was early evening and still light. People were scattered over the village green, finishing off preparations for the following day's Easter Sunday celebrations.

At the pond, two dogs were splashing about at the water's edge, barking and playing tug-of-war over a stick they'd found, while their owners set up temporary bins.

Sylvia passed Hayley a carrier bag of chocolate eggs, unable to miss how angular her daughter's shoulders had got, how thin and dull her long, layered hair was.

Hayley peered into the bag and a flicker of excitement spread over her gaunt features. 'Aren't they pretty? All different sizes and colours. The kids are going to love them.'

Sylvia smiled. She'd got a waft of sweet chocolate. 'You wait. The adults enjoy them too.' She pointed at various spots around them. 'The flags mark the way, look. We need to place the eggs anywhere along the route. Not too high, or the children won't be able to reach them.'

'Right.'

'And we don't "hide" them as such, otherwise they won't find them. They need to be visible.' She reached into the bag she was carrying and brought out a handful of eggs, wrapped in coloured foil.

Hayley watched her mother place one on the roots of a tree and another where a branch joined the main trunk, a foot or so from the ground. She deposited an egg under the arm of a bench, and a couple more amongst some daffodil leaves.

They ambled together, placing eggs and chatting about the Easter egg hunt and the village. Nothing contentious so far.

'How's it been, staying with your gran?' Sylvia put a pink egg on a tuft of grass.

Hayley closed her eyes briefly, as if she was surprised by her grandmother's behaviour. 'She's been brilliant. Asked me a few questions but not pressed me on anything. She loves cooking. I think it's her mission to fatten me up.' She laughed and balanced an egg on a stone that was sticking out of the grass. 'Butter and cream in everything. Puddings. Hot chocolate.'

'I'm glad you're home. We all are.'

Over by the swings, they heard the jangle of bells, shouts and the clack of sticks. Some of the Morris dancers were practising.

'Not sure Dave shares that sentiment but I did suggest he'd killed Lloyd.' Hayley put her mittened hands up to her face. 'I've been angry with him for twenty years.'

Around a tree, several clumps of bluebells were growing fast, not in bloom yet.

Sylvia tucked a couple of eggs amongst the pointed leaves. 'You two will sort things out in time. He reacted because he loves you and thought he was protecting you. It wasn't what *you* wanted so you've been unable to accept that. Massively over-simplifying things but...'

'Put like that, it makes sense. I hadn't realised how much I blamed him.'

'Perhaps it was easier than blaming Lloyd?' Sylvia said gently.

'It's kind of Dave to pay for my therapist. I'm starting with her after Easter.'

'It'll be good to see someone with trauma training.'

Hayley nodded. 'Are you upset I didn't tell you about getting pregnant?'

Sylvia shook her head. 'It's your dad who should've told me. You were a child. None of it was your fault at all.' She paused, choosing her words carefully. 'I regret not knowing, as I would've liked to have got you better support. Looked after you more appropriately.'

'Dad made it sound like I was helping you by not telling you. I didn't question it.'

Sylvia touched Hayley's cheek. 'You had enough on your mind.'

In the Windmill Inn, half an hour later, Dave was waiting for them with Rebus at a table by the fire. He waved. A younger, dark-haired woman was with him.

Sylvia was wondering when Hayley would realise it was her sister.

'I'm going to nip to the loo and wash my hands,' said Hayley.

The bar was filling up. One of the new bar staff was loading wood onto the fire.

'Before you go... I'll get drinks,' said Sylvia. 'What would you like?'

'Could I have a... Is that...?' Hayley glanced from her mum to the table with Dave. '*Karen?*' Hayley dashed over, enveloping her younger sister in a hug.

Chapter 46
SUNDAY

It was Easter Sunday. Ellie woke to the familiar sound of Rebus chewing his paw on the duvet next to her. No kittens pouncing on her hair. No 3am zoomies and dive bombs from the wardrobe.

For now.

And she was back in her own bed.

It had been a strange case and an unsettling week.

Lloyd and Arthur dead. Brendan and Amy in custody. Hayley back home with a referral for psychotherapy for her PTSD. The Durden family could grieve, and so, finally, could Joan's family, safe now from the worry that Lloyd was going to return to the village and torment them. It was difficult finding positives in any murders, but if there had to be one, this was surely it?

But as for Dave... she was still feeling her way through everything that had happened. The secrets and lies. The alien behaviour. They'd all plunged her into a no-man's land of emotions, and she had no idea what lay ahead. There was no big question to answer, as had often been the case in the past. The truth was – she didn't even know what questions to ask.

She imagined him now, waking up down the road at Goose Meadow. Was he pleased to be back home in his flat? She didn't know. Did she wish he was still at the windmill?

In her heart, she knew the answer.

No.

Was that because she no longer loved him? No. It was much more complicated than that.

Her thoughts turned to the families in the village who'd been involved in their investigation. To Amy's mother and aunt. She hoped the two sisters would be able to bury the hatchet and become allies. Lydia had lost her brother and father. Thank goodness she had Barney and her job at the doctor's surgery. They'd have to call round, invite her to events, make sure she was OK.

Her bedroom door nudged open, and Zoe slipped into bed next to her, as she often did.

'Budge up, Reeby,' she said as she tugged at the covers. 'When can we pick up the kittens?'

'I spoke to Fran last night. They can go to their new homes in two weeks.'

Zoe squealed. 'Have you found homes for them all?'

'Yup. Fran's thrilled. Obviously, we're having two. One's going to Leonard at the vicarage, now he's staying on. One to Sally. Lydia's having one. And Sarge wants one.'

'Aww. What about Dad?'

'He's decided against it. Says his shifts are too long.'

'Is he coming to the Easter Egg Hunt?'

'I don't know, sweetie. Text him if you want him to come?'

'I liked it when he was here.' She stuck her bottom lip out in a semi-jokey way.

'I know you did. And I liked aspects of it but not all of it.' She didn't feel able to tell Zoe she'd found it a drain.

'It feels like things are worse between you two now than they've been for a long time.'

Ellie let the comment float about in her head for a few moments. 'Well, I discovered new stuff in a way I didn't like. That took me back to finding out about Andrea.'

'And Gran's annoyed with Grandad *and* Dad. Will you both ever forgive him? Poor Dad.'

Ellie smiled at her daughter. Zoe was learning how messy relationships could be. How little in life was black and white.

'I don't know. People don't like secrets. In the end, they always come out, and people get hurt and lose trust.' She paused as she realised something. 'That's it. I know what's been bothering me. I was starting to trust your dad again.'

'Oh, Mum. I'm so sorry.'

'It's a shame... but I can't ignore it.' Ellie's thoughts drifted to Sylvia admitting she might have been hard on Ron.

'Actually – I'm glad it happened. It's reminded me: there are no guarantees in relationships.' She drummed her fingers on the sheet while she tried to extend the idea in her mind. 'We can ask others to be honest with us but, ultimately, we're responsible for our own happiness.'

'Aww. Mum.' Zoe plonked a kiss on her mother's cheek. 'Auntie Hayley kept a secret too,' she said. 'And Lloyd's father kept the pregnancy a secret from his wife as well.'

The door opened again.

'Thought I heard you chatting. Room for another one?' said Sylvia, in her nightie still.

'We were talking about secrets,' said Zoe.

'Not a fan myself.' Sylvia scrambled in next to Zoe, pushing Rebus out of the way.

'Will Finn keep things from me?'

'I don't know, lovey,' Ellie replied. 'Do you keep them from him?'

'Sometimes. Reeby chewed his t-shirt, and I said it was one of the kittens because I didn't want him to be cross with Rebus. The kittens were tiny, and were going home, so I knew he wouldn't be upset with them.'

'Ah. Lying to protect another.' Sylvia's voice was brittle. 'Or are we lying to protect ourselves?'

'Once I'd said it was the kittens, the lie was out there.'

'We all have to make decisions in the heat of the moment, or when we're bounced into them,' said Sylvia. 'It's not easy. But – we can take them back.' She turned on her side and faced Zoe and Ellie. 'We can say, "I made a mistake".'

'Do you wish Grandad had done that?'

She nodded.

'Why do you think he didn't?'

She shrugged. 'I've been turning that over in my mind. Maybe he was scared. Maybe he thought he'd look weak.'

'Maybe he genuinely thought he'd done the right thing not telling you.' Zoe let her plaits out. 'Mum, when you asked Dad why he lied about having seen Lloyd, he seemed to think his motivations were legit, didn't he?'

'That's true,' replied Ellie. 'I guess there's a difference between doing the right thing and doing something for the right reasons.' She let out a tortured laugh. 'Although where the dividing line is sometimes, who knows? Anyway, that's enough heavy stuff for now. Who's going downstairs to put the kettle on?'

'You are, Mum!' Zoe laughed. 'What time shall we leave for the Bunny Hop? I'm going to text Dad. I don't want him to feel left out.'

'The Morris Dancing starts at ten so a quarter to?'

'I'll text him now.' Zoe fished her phone out from underneath her and started tapping out a message.

The three of them carried on chatting and arguing over who should make the tea.

Zoe's phone beeped.

'It's from Dad.' She read the text aloud.

'You told me to get a hobby – actually, I already did, a few months ago – so I'll be doing that. Have a great day. Love you x'

'He's not coming.' Her voice was flat. 'It won't be the same without him.'

'Wonder what he's doing?' said Ellie. Despite her annoyance with him, she felt something else register in her solar plexus.

Disappointment.

Three hours later, the people of Lower Wootton were assembled on the green. The starting point for the Easter Egg Hunt was here this year with the route around the streets and lanes of the village, so that as many people as possible could take part, even if it was just by standing in the front garden or at the window and waving and cheering.

Over at the pond, Wootton Morris were gathered, ready to dance, wearing white shirts and black breeches, with a crimson waistcoat and a straw hat. The squire shouted his command and the accordion started its rousing tune.

'Let's watch the dancing,' said Sylvia, and she, Ellie and Zoe drifted over, along with lots of other people.

After a number of foot stamps and hollers, each man in the side stood in a line opposite another man. They banged long sticks with the person opposite, three times at head height and three times lower. Then leaped in the air, bells rattling on the pads on their shins, linking their free arms and spinning round.

The crowd cheered.

Zoe squealed. '*It's Dad*. Mum, look.' She pointed.

The men released arms, danced four steps back and four steps forward.

Dave bashed sticks with the man opposite, over their heads, skipped forwards a few steps and backwards again.

'This is a surprise,' Ellie shouted over the noise.

The accordion player started to sing, and a fiddle joined in.

'You wanted him to have a hobby,' Sylvia yelled to Zoe.

'Yeah, but...'

Dave was smiling.

Handkerchiefs now replaced sticks. With a flourish of white cloth over their heads, the Morris men swooped backwards and forwards, stamped their feet and hollered. Spun round, bells jangling, hollered again.

'Not bad, is he?' said Nick, the butcher, as he joined them. 'For a copper.' He laughed. 'Enjoying it too. I'm proud of him. But the boys at the nick have been giving him hell.'

Once the dancing was finished, the stalls and stands opened. All set up on the green, with activities scheduled to run until 4pm. Ellie and Sylvia wandered round, chatting to friends and inspecting their offerings.

Kathy from the bakery was selling simnel cake and hot cross buns, which she and Sylvia had made. Sally and her partner were decorating Easter biscuits with a family. Zoe and Finn each had a child in a chair for face painting, and a queue of customers waiting excitedly.

Staff from the village school were doing egg painting. Ellie's favourite, run by a couple from a neighbouring village, was the 'hold an owl' stall.

On the next stand, the owner of the knitting and pattern shop had teamed up with Helen the hairdresser. People could buy and decorate an Easter bonnet with flowers and ribbon.

'Oh, wow.' Ellie turned to Sylvia. 'Let's get bonnets.' She smiled at Helen. 'Two please. And Happy Easter.'

Sylvia chose a straw bonnet; Ellie, a black top hat. They selected leaves, twigs and flowers. Sylvia attached a lace ribbon to hers and stitched violets, forget-me-nots and wood anemones in place. Ellie glued a fluffy, yellow, toy chick to the brim and band of her topper, adding pink bunny ears and a daffodil.

They pulled their hats on and looked at each other, laughing. Helen snapped a picture to put on the village Facebook page.

Over by the pond, the Morris dancers were packing away. Some passed jugs of ale, in line with tradition. Others swigged water and chatted.

Ellie felt the tug of guilt in her stomach. The gnaw of bad feeling that'd been left unresolved.

Dave and Nick were chatting when she reached them. Dave had his back to her.

'This the new hobby?' she said warmly. 'You were very good.'

He spun round. 'Ells. Oh – nice hat.' He grinned at her. 'Can't believe how much fun it is. Been doing it since Christmas but wish I'd started years ago.'

Sylvia joined Ellie, then Zoe too.

'I'm really sorry about keeping stuff from you. It was... wrong.' Dave's eyes were wide, sincere and open. 'I can learn. I'll learn. I *can*.'

Ellie leant forward and gave him a hug. As her cheek touched his, her hat tumbled.

Zoe lunged forward and grabbed it.

'I know,' Ellie told him. '*I'm* sorry too. And I've got some learning to do as well.'

After lunch, it was the Easter Egg Hunt. Children with painted faces, adults and dogs, stood at the brightly decorated HOP THIS WAY sign, ready to go, excitedly clasping a clue sheet and map in one hand and a basket, bucket or pail to put their hidden treasure in, in the other.

Tied to a tree, a poster detailed all the prizes. Large, coloured arrows pointed the way.

Ellie surveyed the crowd. They hadn't had this many people for a few years. She took in the costumes. A father with silk bunny ears on his head. Someone in a full-length white rabbit costume. A baby dressed as an egg. A Labrador with a rabbit tail. Balloons floated above pushchairs, pastel colours, like painted eggs.

The 'Easter Bunny' – a local person in costume whose identity was being kept a secret – was about to count down. In a silly voice, he told the children to have fun and said there were plenty of eggs for everyone. 'We'll see you all back here in half an hour for a surprise, and to feed the lambs.'

A cheer went up.

'FIVE, FOUR, THREE, TWO, ONE, GO!' he shouted.

Despite his attempts to disguise his voice, it was familiar, but Ellie couldn't place it.

Amidst much squealing and laughter, the groups set off, some dashing this way and that, others ambling at a more leisurely speed.

Ellie, Sylvia and Zoe stood, arms linked, watching as the village green became a mass of yellow and white blobs, all of different sizes, moving across the grass towards Pennypot Lane. Not everyone was here, of course. Joan, Arthur and Lloyd. Amy and Brendan. But hopefully their family and friends were together.

Half an hour later, the egg hunt was over and it was time to 'meet the Easter Bunny'.

'We've included an extra special feature today,' the Easter Bunny told them. 'I understand it's not been an easy time in the village lately. So, before we feed the lambs, we're going to announce the results of the Springwatch Photography Competition.'

He fished under his costume and retrieved a piece of paper. 'In third place, receiving a voucher for £50, we have Joshua Simmons, with a beautiful close-up shot of new growth on an ash tree.'

Clapping.

'In second place, receiving a voucher for £100, it's Lucy Reynolds with a ground level shot of wood anemones in dappled sunlight.'

Clapping and cheers.

'In first place, we have Zoe Blix with an incredible shot of hares boxing in a beautiful meadow, orange dawn light streaming onto the pond behind them.'

'You're kidding,' Zoe shouted.

'Congratulations,' the man said. 'You win a place on my nature photography course.'

'*My?* Is that–'

He unzipped his bunny costume and pulled the hood back.

'It's *Chris Flipping Packham.*' Zoe ran over to him. 'Thank you, thank you so much. I can't believe it... I...'

'Bit of a relief to get out of that costume, I can tell you,' said Chris. 'I'm sweating like anything. You are very welcome. How did you get the light like that? I'm interested to know what shutter speed you...'

'Well.' It was Dave. 'That's rather nice, isn't it?'

'Did you know he was coming?'

'I couldn't possibly say.'

'Now, ladies and gents, children and animals,' said Chris. 'If I can steer you towards the pen over by the pond, we are going to see some of the village's lambs, and those who want to feed them, can.'

The local farmer let down the back of his trailer and ten lambs skipped down the slope onto the grass, followed by his collie. The dog deftly herded the lambs into the pen and the farmer closed it.

Leonard had arrived with Sarge, and the two of them were standing by the enclosure sipping cups of ginger wine. Sylvia joined them, with Ellie and Dave following.

'We're having a roast later, if you'd like to come,' Ellie told Dave. 'Zoe and Finn are doing it. We'd love you to join us.'

'Oh?' He sounded surprised. 'I'd like that. Thank you.'

'Zoe's invited Mary and Hayley. If Karen can get the kids sorted, she's coming too, and Sylvia's invited Leonard and Sarge. So, if you're up for a crowd, it'll be fun.'

He nodded. 'I've had an apology from the chief super by the way. He rang me last night.'

'Good.'

'And I've spoken to Mum.'

'She told me,' Ellie replied. 'No more secrets, eh?'

'I promise,' he whispered. 'No more secrets.'

Ellie heard the conviction in his voice; saw it in his eyes. But, however much Dave meant it, the tests would come. And in those hard moments, would he be able to stick to it?

Surely it was best to leave him to worry about that? Because – even if he never lied to her again; never kept anything from her again, unless she worked on her trust issues, and stopped asking 'what if?', she would never be able to let him – or anyone else – in again.

With her family and friends around her, and the home and village she adored, perhaps she could practise trusting... without guarantees.

She'd done it before. She could do it again, couldn't she?

The End.

If you enjoyed Ellie, Zoe and Sylvia's story in this book, follow their adventures in the next one, *Murder at the Summer Swim*, which is available on Amazon here.

A poisoned chemist. A family vineyard under threat. Three women sleuths.

Ellie Blix was craving a quiet summer, but documentary-makers have descended on the windmill and are causing chaos.

Then, a local is found dead on her towel at the end of the annual barbecue on the beach, and the village is plunged into shock. The dead woman is a former chemistry teacher from the local school who has just beaten seasoned professionals in a prestigious wine-making prize.

When Ellie's daughter, Zoe, learns her favourite teacher recently received a sinister parcel, she's sure the death is suspicious, and is determined to investigate.

Then an anonymous caller reveals shattering information on local radio about the windmill's history, and Ellie wonders if there's a connection between her family home and the murder on the beach.

But who is the caller? And what secret agreements did the historic windmill owners have?

When a second parcel is received by Ellie herself, she realises that Blix Investigators have fallen for a deadly trap. And the killer is closing in....

Order *Murder at the Summer Swim* here.

A note from the author

Dear reader,

Thank you so much for reading this book. It has been a pleasure to write but, without you, it would simply be words in a document on my hard drive.

It is immensely gratifying that so many of you have taken the characters and stories from *The Wootton Windmill Mysteries* into your homes and hearts. Many of you have taken the time to email and tell me what the stories have meant to you. I read and reply to each one.

Getting news first

The best way to keep in touch is to join my newsletter. This is where I share news first, including exclusive offers, early reads, 'behind the scenes' & giveaways. You can join here.

Supporting the series

You can do this in three ways:

a) If you've enjoyed this story, please tell your friends, family, book clubs, and online groups about the series. It's easy to underestimate what this can do, but word of mouth is one of the best forms of marketing.

b) Another way to help is by leaving a quick, written review on Amazon. Amazon prompts us to leave a rating when we finish a book on kindle, and the average rating is important. However, a few lines saying what you liked about the story helps other readers to know what the book is like.

c) By pre-ordering the next in the series, which you can do here.

Please note: I am a British writer and I write using British English. This story is set in an English village and the manuscript has been edited and proofread by British professionals. A few spellings, terms and words may, therefore, be different for some readers. I've tried to ensure, however, that the meaning is clear for everyone. In addition, the stories are intended to be lighthearted reads. They aren't police procedurals and the sleuths do things detectives aren't allowed to do. This is intentional and is meant to be part of the fun of a cosy mystery.

I get a lot of emails and messages asking me if Lower Wootton is a real place. It isn't. sorry. It is a fictional village which I've created by borrowing elements of many villages, mixing them up and fictionalising them. If you try to plot places, you will find I've moved them, changed them and given them different names!

Finally, writing a novel is a team effort. I come up with the plot and characters, and write the words, and other people contribute at various stages. Without their input and magic, this story would not have made it into print.

I owe massive thanks to the following people for their help. In no particular order: Lynne Nazareth, Scott Pack, Louise Voss, Ken Dawson, Imran Mahmood, Lucy Lawrie, Anne Coates. Linda and Alan Standen for very generous help when Lexi and I had surgery. Thanks also to Liz and Keith Atkinson who own Ripple Windmill, the inspiration for Ellie, Sylvia and Zoe's home in the series. To all my early and beta readers.

Sincere apologies to anyone I've forgotten.

About the author

Izzie Harper is the pen name of British writer, teacher & story coach, Vicky Newham. Vicky lives on the south coast of England.

As Izzie Harper, she writes *The Wootton Windmill Mysteries*.

Vicky's first crime fiction series was published by HQ/Harper Collins. Her debut in this police procedural series, *Turn a Blind Eye*, was optioned for TV and was shortlisted for the CWA John Creasey Debut Dagger in 2019. She has MAs in Creative Writing and Effective Learning.

To keep up to date with Vicky's releases, special offers and promotions, please join her newsletter here.

If you like pictures of dogs, the sea, the Kent countryside and behind-the-scenes of Vicky's writing, you can follow her on Twitter at @VickyNewham and on Instagram at @vickynewhamwriter.

If you have enjoyed this story, Vicky would be hugely grateful if you could leave a quick review on Amazon and if you could tell your family and friends about it. Reviews and word-of-mouth recommendations are the best way to help authors.

And, please pre-order book 5, *Murder at the Summer Swim*, here.

Made in United States
Troutdale, OR
06/13/2024

20510901R10224